I0615542

John Murphy

Solemnities of the dedication and opening of the Catholic

University of America

November 13, 1889, official report

John Murphy

Solemnities of the dedication and opening of the Catholic University of America
November 13, 1889, official report

ISBN/EAN: 9783741183171

Manufactured in Europe, USA, Canada, Australia, Japa

Cover: Foto ©Andreas Hilbeck / pixelio.de

Manufactured and distributed by brebook publishing software
(www.brebook.com)

John Murphy

Solemnities of the dedication and opening of the Catholic

University of America

DIVINITY COLLEGE OF THE CATHOLIC UNIVERSITY OF AMERICA.

DEUS LUX MEA.

SOLEMNITIES

OF THE

DEDICATION AND OPENING

OF THE

CATHOLIC UNIVERSITY OF AMERICA.

November 13th, 1889.

OFFICIAL REPORT.

BALTIMORE:
JOHN MURPHY & CO.
1890.

INDEX.

4

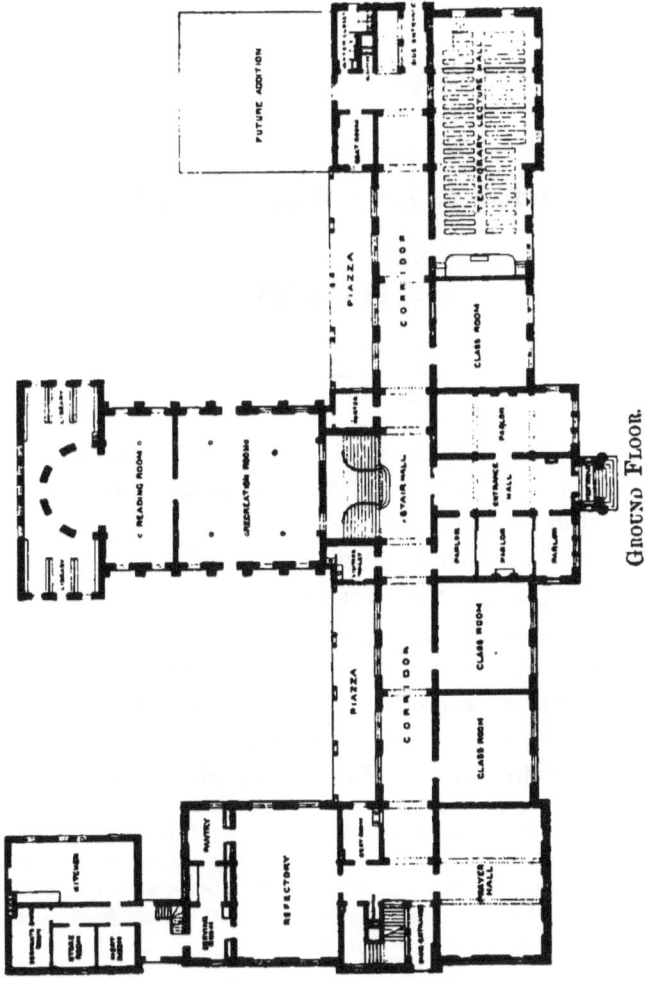

GROUND FLOOR.

INAUGURATION

OF THE

CATHOLIC UNIVERSITY

OF

AMERICA.

THE first centenary of the Hierarchy in the United States was fittingly crowned by the inauguration of the Catholic University of America. Our Holy Father, Pope Leo XIII, in his Apostolic Letter of March 7th, 1889, notes the relation between these two events. "In this matter," he says, "we deem most worthy of all praise your intention of inaugurating the University during the centenary of the establishment of the Ecclesiastical Hierarchy in your country, as a monument and perpetual memorial of that most auspicious event."[1] The

---

[1] "Qua in re omni laude dignissimum judicamus consilium vestrum, qui anno centesimo ab ecclesiastica hierarchia istic constituta, monumentum ac memoriam perpetuam rei auspicatissimae, initiis Universitati positis, statuere decrevistis."— *S. D. N. Leonis Papae XIII epistola de Magno Lycaeo Catholico Foederatorum Americae Septentrionalis Statuum, in Urbe Washington constituto.*

1

happy coincidence thus alluded to by his Holiness was an incentive which powerfully spurred on the work of preparation and secured its accomplishment in due time. An army of workmen were engaged on the building up to the very eve of the dedication; but when the eventful day dawned, all was in readiness, the structure was richly and tastefully decorated from ground-floor to roof, the chapel, with its thirteen altars, was exquisitely adorned, the Professors and most of the students were already lodged in their apartments, ready to receive and welcome the host of expected guests.

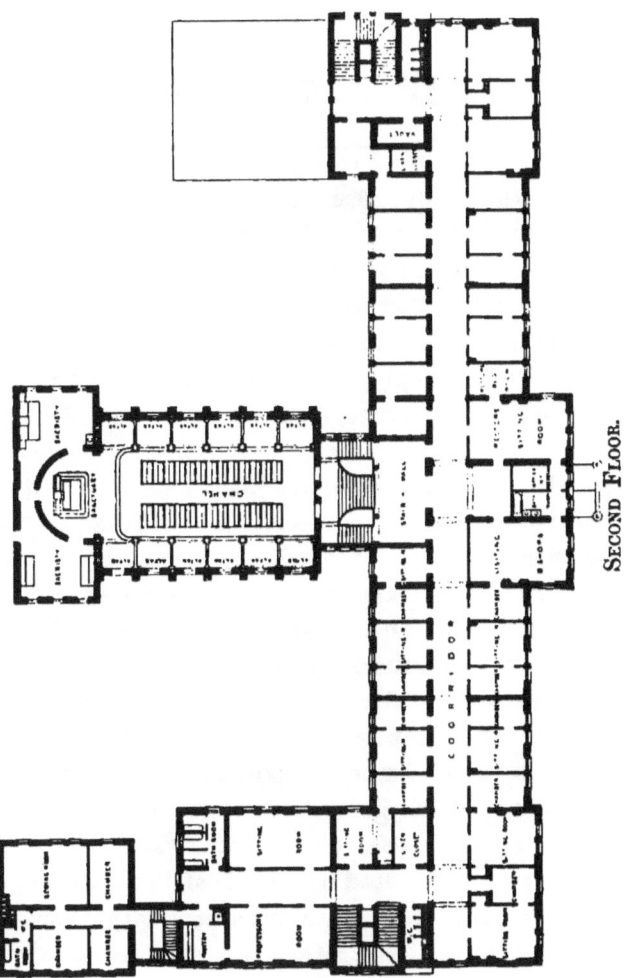

SECOND FLOOR.

I.

THE DEDICATION.

Wednesday, Nov. 13th, 1889, witnessed the dedication of the University to Almighty God and the formal opening of its courses of instruction. A heavy rain fell during the whole forenoon; but the multitudes in attendance still numbered thousands, and the solemnity of the occasion was scarcely, if at all, impaired. The grand assemblage of the Archbishops and Bishops of the United States, with their brethren from Canada, Mexico, and England, who had so splendidly celebrated the centenary in Baltimore, came by a special train to take part in the inauguration of the University. And with them were united Prelates, Vicars General, Superiors and Provincials of Religious Orders and Congregations, Heads of Universities, Seminaries and Colleges, Reverend Clergy, and Ecclesiastical Students, from every part of the country, to the number of at least six hundred. The laity in countless numbers flocked to the scene, and filled the building and the grounds throughout the day.

Shortly after 10.30, the solemn strains of the *Veni Creator Spiritus*, chanted by a choir of two hundred and fifty seminarians from St. Mary's Seminary, Baltimore, and St. Charles' College, Maryland, with accompaniment

3

by the Marine Band, floated through the building and announced the opening of the ceremonies. At the close of the hymn, his Eminence, Cardinal Gibbons, Chancellor of the University, attended by the usual ministers and acolytes, solemnly blessed and dedicated the Divinity Chapel, under the patronage and title of St. Paul, the Apostle of the Gentiles, who had been chosen, with the approbation of the Holy See, as the Patron of the Faculty of Divinity. The Psalms and Litany of this impressive ceremony were chanted by the same choir of ecclesiastical students, the responses being sung by the imposing throng of dignitaries and clergy who filled every corner of the Chapel. The effect was majestic and thrilling in the extreme.

THE PONTIFICAL MASS.

As soon as the rite of dedication was finished, his Eminence, Cardinal Gibbons, went to his throne on the Gospel side of the sanctuary, a similar throne on the Epistle side being occupied by his Eminence, Cardinal Taschereau, Archbishop of Quebec, and the solemn Mass of the Holy Ghost was begun. The celebrant of the Mass was the Most Rev. Monsignor Francesco Satolli, Archbishop of Lepanto, who had been sent by the Sovereign Pontiff, to show by his presence at the centenary and the inauguration the deep and affectionate interest felt by the Holy Father in these two memorable events. It was well known that he had been selected for this high duty, not only on account of the special friendship deservedly entertained for him by the Holy Father, but also because of his being the living embodiment of those views and aspirations in regard to higher learning, which have given such special lustre to the pontificate of Leo XIII. Nothing, therefore, could have been more appropriate and impressive than the spectacle of such a man, the representative of the Vicar of Christ himself, surrounded by that imposing assemblage of the highest dignitaries of the Church in America, standing at the high altar of the newly dedicated chapel, to offer up the Divine Mysteries in supplication for the guidance of the Spirit of Truth upon all the future work of the University. In this august function he was most appropriately assisted by sacred ministers selected from among his former pupils at the American College in Rome, while the universally esteemed Rector of the College, Rt. Rev. Monsignor O'Connell, assisting at the right of Cardinal Gibbons, gave additional testimony to the bonds of sympathy and affection which unite these two homes of highest learning in effort for the welfare of their common country.

The Faculty of the University occupied posts of honor immediately after those of the Archbishops and Bishops, while the students mingled with their brethren of the clergy who filled the corridors and halls, unable to obtain room within the limits of the chapel. A small number of the laity, founders of Chairs and other principal benefactors of the University, had seats reserved for them. The music of the Mass, which excited the admiration of all present, was rendered by a select choir of male singers, under the direction of Rev. Joseph Graf, the University choir-master.

At the end of the Pontifical Mass, the Dedicatory Sermon was preached by the Rt. Rev. Bishop of Cleveland, as follows:

SERMON

DELIVERED BY THE

RT. REV. R. GILMOUR, D. D.,

BISHOP OF CLEVELAND.

When men erect buildings and establish institutions, the public has a right to know for what they are to be used. The widespread notice given the ceremony of to-day, and the earnestness of all connected with the work, show the deep interest taken by the public in this Catholic University; nor without cause, for within this building principles are to be taught and minds formed in whose future American society is deeply interested. Knowledge and doctrine will therefore be the objective work of this institution.

The quest for knowledge began with the human race, and the progress of arts and science is written on every page of history. The acquisitions of primeval man were carried into the ark, and afterwards gave direction to the daring that would build a tower whose ruins are the wonder of the modern archæologist. In the hieroglyphics of Egypt is written the advance of science, and in the ruins of Thebes and Babylon the strength of thought.

In the schools of Athens was found the polish of Greece, and in the wisdom of Cato the strength of Rome. Saul drank in knowledge in the schools of the prophets, whilst the poetry of David and the eloquence of Isaias teach us that others than Homer and Demosthenes were masters of speech. Solomon was taught of God, while Moses was instructed in all the knowledge of Egypt. The eloquence of Paul and the polish of John bespeak the literary culture of the Jew, while Jerusalem, with its temple of unparalleled beauty, tells the limit art and science had reached. Knowledge made Babylon strong, Greece cultured, and Rome mistress of the world.

Civilization is limited only by education. The civilization of this nineteenth century is but the accumulated results of the world's history. The serpent tempted Eve with the offer of knowledge, and the limit was: "Ye shall be as gods, knowing good and evil."

The appetite for knowledge is ceaseless, and its possession but increases its capacity for more. It is also a significant fact that from the beginning religion and education have been linked hand in hand. "Ye shall be as gods," says the serpent; "Find knowledge at the lips of the priest," say the Scriptures; "Go teach," says Christ to His apostles.

The motive that has brought here to-day the chief magistrate of this great republic, and these high dignitaries of church and state, and this distinguished audience of the laity, is worthy of deepest thought. Kind friends! you are not here to assist at the dedication of this fair building—classic in its lights and shades of art—to the mere cultivation of the arts and sciences, valuable though they are. A higher motive has brought you here, and a higher motive prompted the first munificent gift and subsequent generosity that have rendered this institution possible. This building has just been blessed and forever dedicated to the cultivation of the science of sciences —the knowledge of God. It was well to have begun with the Divinity department, if for nothing else than to teach that all true education must begin in God and find its truth and direction in God.

Education has for its motive the fitting and directing of man in his relations to God and society. Man is not for himself. He was created for a higher and a nobler purpose. All things, from the universe to the grain of sand on the sea shore, exist for the benefit of others. In God, creation was not necessary: however, God has created that He might bless, and creation is but the extension of His first beneficence. God is not for Himself; man is not for himself; society is not for itself; the state is not for itself; the Church is not for itself.

There are two orders of society, the spiritual and the temporal. They are both of God, and have their rights and duties for the weal of man. In much they are separate and independent; in much they are conjoint and correlative. Man is composed of body and soul, so society is composed of the moral and the physical. The function of the state is to deal with the physical; the duty of religion is to deal with the moral. As in man the body is for the soul and the soul for the body, so in society religion is for the state and the state for religion.

Their conjoint work is for God and man. God is glorified in man, and man is made happy in God, and this conjoint work—the glory of God and happiness of man is the objective work of religion and state. In this is found the motive for their existence, the origin of their authority, and their right to man's obedience. They represent God, and each in its sphere is the expression of God to man. We obey the state because the state represents God in the temporal: "By me kings reign and princes have their power." We accept religion because religion represents God in the spiritual: "He that heareth you heareth Me."

God leaves to society the right to determine its form of government and who shall be its rulers; God leaves to the Church the determination and management of the human in her. In neither is God or God's law responsible for the human in them. In the human both depend on human prudence for their success. In the light of these principles the state is free to change its form of government, as is also religion free to change its policy in human affairs. But the state is not free to deny God or discard His law, nor is religion free to change what is divine. Both are from God and in the things of God are immutable.

There is a widespread mistake, a rapidly growing political and social heresy which assumes and asserts that the state is all temporal, and religion all spiritual. This is not only a doctrinal heresy, but if acted on would end in ruin to both spiritual and temporal. No more can the state exist without religion than can the body exist without the soul, and no more can religion exist without the state and, on earth, carry on its work, than can the soul, on earth, without the body do its work. The state, it is true, is for the temporal, but has its substantial strength in the moral, while religion, it is true, is for the spiritual, but in much must find its working strength in the temporal. In this sense it is a mistake to assume that religion is independent of the state, or the state independent of religion. As a matter of fact religion must depend upon the state in temporals, and *vice versa* the state must depend upon religion in morals, and both should so act that their conjoint work will be the temporal and moral welfare of society.

The morality of the citizen is the real strength of the state, but the teaching of morality is the function of religion and in so much is religion necessary to the state. In this sense it is foolish to assert that religion is independent of the state, or the state is independent of religion, or that they can, or ought to be separated, one from the other.

In this country we have agreed that religion and the state shall exist as distinct and separate departments, each with its separate rights and duties, but this does not mean that the state is independent of religion, or religion independent of the state. God is as necessary for the state as He is necessary for religion. No state can exist, or should exist, that does not recognize God as the supreme authority. So far no state, Pagan or Christian, has attempted to rule without a god, false or true, but a god, and a god's law have been accepted in every society as the origin and basis of the state's authority. Woe be

to the state that denies God, or attempts to govern society without God and God's law. Brute force is tyranny;
moral force is reason. Man must be governed by reason,
not by force, and the state will find its true strength in
the morality of the citizen. God is the strength of the
state, the guide of the citizen and the protection of society.

In the past, states, Pagan or Christian, have been
strong in proportion as their conception of God was strong,
and in proportion to the vigor of their moral laws. Israel
grew and prevailed in proportion as she kept God's law.
Rome and Greece were strong because their conception
of God was strong. Mohammedanism lives in its god
rather than in its prophet, and Buddha and Brahma
hold their own against the world. In proportion as
Christianity has been accepted have science and civilization progressed. God is the power in law, and law is the
guide in morals, and morals are the strength of society.
Hence religion must support the state and teach the citizen obedience to legitimate authority. "Thou shalt not
kill," "thou shalt not steal," "thou shalt not commit
adultery," are of more value to the state than all its
armies or navies combined.

American society has been strong because we are and
have been a religious people. Our colonies were founded
by men pre-eminently religious. Our laws and constitu-
tions are the outgrowth of the Christian law. We are
strong because our faith in God is strong, and we will live
and strengthen in proportion as we are guided by His law.

In the light of the above fundamental and all-important truths it is not difficult to see how valuable Christian

education is to society. Education refines society, elevates man and directs all to the higher good. No nobler mission than that of a teacher; by office a leader, by talent an inventor, and by genius an originator and director of power.

Gioja of Amalfi, gave the mariner's compass; Columbus, America; Watt, the steam engine, and Morse the telegraph; and these four men have revolutionized the material world. The single thought: "No man shall be oppressed for conscience sake," has given more peace and security to society than all the armies of the world; and that other thought: "All men are created free and equal," has given a continent its political life.

Now, in the light of these grave and fundamental truths the question naturally arises, "What are the end and scope of a university?" a question that will be answered according as we understand the end and mission of the educator.

Education is a grave and serious matter. On its character society rises or falls, advances or recedes. The true end of education is to elevate the human race, purify morals, and direct society to a higher perfection. Education must therefore embrace science and religion, the former to increase human happiness, the latter to direct man to his true end. Now the end of man is "to glorify God, and enjoy Him forever," or, in the language of philosophy, "to seek for the true and the good."

Man was made for growth. Creation is progressive. Nothing stands still. All flows on, like the current of a deep and mighty river, bidding man look forward and

upward; increasing knowledge, deepening thought, puri-
fying morals, and directing all to God, the only good.

The end, then, of a university is to gather within its
halls the few who are brighter in intellect and keener in
thought, and to expand and vivify within them knowledge; then send them forth leaders to instruct and train
the masses. Knowledge is not for its possessor, nor
genius for the individual. Both are gifts from God to be
used for the general good. No greater mistake than for
the scholar or the school to assume that knowledge is for
himself, or itself. The scholar belongs to neither race
nor country. His home is the world, his pupil, man, and
his reward, God. His mission is to know truth, and then
fearlessly proclaim it. He is not to take from the masses
nor swim with the current. Like the general of an army,
he must strike home fearlessly where ignorance or evil
exists. God has made him a leader, genius has gifted
him with power, and he must not falter or fail in the high
mission entrusted to him.

The tendency of the age is to level down, to make
smatterers instead of thinkers. Perhaps not since the
days of Plato and Cicero has there been less depth of
thought than at present. Education has increased in
quantity, but lessened in quality. To teach our young to
read and write, and fit our youth for the counting room
is the limit of our common school. To teach men to
think, or to direct men to God, is not in the curriculum
of modern education. To break away from the past is
the monomania of the day, and he who does that most
recklessly is the Star in the East. Amid this general

leveling down and breaking away we have but faint
echoes and fewer voices standing for the truth or giving
sturdy blows to error.

The value of a trained special education was markedly
shown in our late desperate war. No braver men ever
entered an army than our volunteer soldiers, and in the
beginning it was difficult to say who was the better, the
volunteer or the trained officer. But as the struggle went
on the names of the soldiers educated in the science of
war rose, and in their success showed clearly the value of
the higher military training they had received. The
same is seen in the medical and legal professions. And
the same is pre-eminently seen in the clerical profession.
As a rule men will not be scholars other than by labored
study. Having widened the circle of popular education
it becomes a necessity to increase the centers of higher
education. We have Harvard and Yale in the non-
Catholic world, Georgetown and Notre Dame in the
Catholic world, all doing yeoman's duty in their line.
But the centers for a higher education are entirely too
few in the country. Much has been done, much is doing,
but much remains to be done, to train the few to be
leaders.

The education of the masses has up to this formed
amongst us the great task of church and state. With
our independence came the readjustment of society in the
light of our religious and civil liberty. Animosities had
to be abated, new thoughts created, a wilderness cleared,
and a home for the world provided. As Catholics, poverty and limited numbers left us crippled, and the ter-

rific struggle to provide lodging and religious attendance
for the immigrant, estopped the possibility of higher
education. Added to this was the organization of the
public schools which Catholics could not in conscience
use, thus imposing upon them the unjust burden of building for themselves and supporting separate schools,
whilst they are taxed for the public schools. Catholics
have no contention with the public schools, because they
are public schools, nor because they are state schools ;
nor do Catholics seek to destroy the public schools. On
the contrary, Catholics are willing to accept the public
schools in America as they have done in Europe and
elsewhere, on condition that an arrangement be made by
which the child shall be taught religion and the laws of
morality.

Our 650 colleges and academies, 3,100 parish schools,
27 seminaries for the training of the clergy, and two universities, are a glorious galaxy amid which to plant this
Catholic University ; perhaps the first great university of
the world begun without state or princely aid, but origi-
nating in the outpouring of Catholic thought, and founded
and provided for by the gifts of the many as well as by
the offerings of the few. It bespeaks the widening character of American thought and the existing conviction of
the public mind that a line of higher studies is clearly
needed.

In the school and college the many are to be taught,
but in the university the few. Here statesmen and
churchmen are to be prepared and through them the
masses moulded and society guided. It was therefore

wise that this University should begin with the Divinity
department, thus teaching that the true beginning of all
things is God; that on Him depend life, liberty, and
happiness, and without Him there can be no permanent
success in church or state. God is the basis of society;
God is essential to success.

As a people we have undertaken the great and wise
task of educating the masses and as far as in us lies, providing that no child within this land shall fail to know
how to read and write. So far, so good, and for the aver-
age man and woman this is enough. But society needs
more than this. Society needs leaders, educated men and
women. This our common school does not give, cannot
give, and never was intended, or should be intended to
give. Scholars are made in colleges and universities.
Now, I hold, no money expended by church or state is of
greater value to society than that expended in founding
and maintaining colleges and universities and providing
a higher education for the talented of all classes. The
trend of the day is to the accumulation of wealth. A
much more healthy trend will be, to train minds, and
create thinkers, who will be as a breakwater against the
domination of wealth. This is needed to stay in measure
the licentiousness of our times, and the radicalism with
which society is threatened. Knowledge is better than
wealth, and intelligence is the only true source of power.
Enlightened by human knowledge and guided by divine
law, man is impregnable and society safe.

In the curriculum of this Catholic University the best
in each of the several branches will be adopted, and in

the light of European and American experience improved upon. In the Divinity Class a broad and suggestive ' course will be given, including the best in past and present. In this line science and revelation will be harmonized, doubt dispelled and truth vindicated. In the department of philosophy the statesman will find the principles of government, and in history the causes for success and the reasons for failure. In law the good of the past will be retained and its imperfections rejected. In this an effort should be made to lay aside the useless and the obsolete. The world changes and has changed; so should law change to suit the changed condition of times and places. This is especially needed in ecclesiastical law.

In this light specialists will come to this university, one to study Divinity, another Scripture, or History, while others will take up Law and Medicine. Here the philologist and scientist will find the best, and all will find their noblest aspirations enlarged and spurred on to the full.

Make these higher studies popular. Let generosity mark the spirit of this house of learning. Let its halls be filled with the best of our youth, and let every effort be made to place this University in the front ranks of modern institutions of learning. But above all, let no narrowness seek to make this the only Catholic University in this country. We have broad lands and eager hearts elsewhere, who in time will need new centers. Let the great ambition of this University be to lead in all that tends to elevate our race, benefit our fellow-citizens, and bless our country.

Revelation is God's best gift to man. The mission of this University is to take up all that is good in human knowledge, purify it in the alembic of God's revelation, and give it back to man blessed in the light of God's truth, increased in volume and intensified in force, thus giving science its direction and revelation its complement.

While the distinguished audience in the chapel were listening to the discourse of the Bishop of Cleveland, an eager multitude of clergy and laity filled the lecture-hall and the adjacent corridor, to hear the renowned Passionist, Father Fidelis, long known and admired as the Rev. James Kent Stone. His sermon was as follows:

THE VITALITY OF THE CHURCH A MANIFESTATION OF GOD.

DISCOURSE DELIVERED

By REV. FATHER FIDELIS, C. P.

"Not unto us, O Lord, not unto us, but unto Thy name give glory, for Thy mercy and for Thy truth's sake; lest the Gentiles should say: Where is their God?" (*Ps.* cxiii, 9, 10.)

My Christian Friends and Fellow-Countrymen :—

This is a day for us, not so much of effort in the initiation of a great work, but rather of wonder and thanksgiving, whilst we contemplate the things which the Omnipotent God has done for us and among us. It is ours to gaze upon the evolution of God's plan, becoming intelligible before our eyes. It is ours to stand still a moment, to stand like the rescued people of old, and behold what God hath wrought. We have been brought out of a land of bondage. Our fathers passed over the Red Sea of obstruction which girdled them round as with despair. They were led through the weary wilderness of trial and patient waiting. And now we, their children, have come into a goodly land, into this land of promise, into a plenteous inheritance. Here may we sit at ease, each under his vine and fig tree, with none to make us afraid, whilst roundabout on every side the old walled cities of antique prejudice are silently crumbling, as at the touch of an unseen hand. Well may we raise our hearts to-day in solemn rejoicing, and break into the oft-sung words of the psalm of deliverance: "When Israel came out of Egypt, the House of Jacob from a barbarous people, Judea was made His sanctuary, Israel His dominion. The sea saw and fled, Jordan was driven back. At the presence of the Lord the earth was moved, at the presence of the God of Jacob, who turned the rock into pools of water and the stony hill into fountains of water. Not unto us, O Lord, not unto us, but unto Thy name give glory, for Thy mercy and for Thy truth's sake."

I shall not attempt, my friends, on this occasion any formal or academic discourse fit for the opening of a new university. I leave this task for those to whom it rightly belongs and to those who speak with authority. We stand only on the skirts of the assembly which has gath-

ered together to honor this festal day. I address you,
therefore, as one of yourselves, as one of the multitude,
whilst I ask you to follow me in a few reflections which
will be but the carrying out of the idea already touched
on in your hearing, as seeming to be the natural and
irrepressible keynote of this harmonious celebration. I
offer you this thought, that the vitality of the Catholic
Church is a manifestation of God; that the spectacle of
the Church's life and work, her majestic development,
carries with it the conviction that the Almighty is opera-
ting by her and in her, and that the finger of God is here.
I shall not endeavor to prove this as a proposition, but
rather to bring it home to you as a fact. Scholastic dis-
sertation on such a subject would be not merely out of
place, it would be to fall below the level of our theme,
and to treat as a dead theorem what we would rather
gaze at as a living reality. We are not discussing a
doctrine; we are contemplating a great, a divine exhibi-
tion; it is there, before us; if we will but open the eyes
of our mind to behold it, we can catch its outlines loom-
ing out on the slow-moving canvas of time. And it will
be mine to-day simply to point you to the picture, and
then to leave you to your own meditations.

My friends, the only hope for humanity is that there
is *somewhere* a revelation, a manifestation of God in time,
a coming in of the Infinite into this world of ours. The
woes of our race are too real, too deep, too inveterate to
be healed by any but a Divine touch. And yet the world
goes on, blindly seeking some outlet from its misery
where, alas! there is none; it dreams fever-dreams of

happiness, and starts up to find its condition more hope-
less than before. Century after century passes, and still
the "hungry generations" push each other on, and the
cry of desperation grows wilder as civilization becomes
more elaborate. You believe in a God, do you not? (I
speak to those here present who may not be Catholics.)
Yes, I know you do, though sometimes you may have
been tempted to doubt Him. Better an infinite personal
Spirit, directing all things in spite of apparent contradiction and imperfection, than a blind impersonal force, whirl-
ing us onward, we know not whither. Materialism is too de-
grading a doctrine to be held by men conscious of the dignity of their own spiritual powers; it could find an advocacy
only in those baser passions of our nature which would rise
up to dethrone spirit, and with it truth and right and moral
responsibility. Yes, you believe in God, you believe in
Him rather than know Him; and this belief has been to
you a solace in the midst of much that is dark and per-
plexing. It has gone before you, like the pillar of fire
and cloud, of fire by night and cloud by day, brighter,
more distinct, in the darkness of silence and sorrow that
shuts out the landscape of this world, yet still there amid
the activity of daily life, an obscure majestic column,
pointing towards heaven. But if you believe in God,
you cannot doubt that He has given us a Revelation,
aye, and more than a Revelation, that He has come to
the rescue of His creatures, and supplied them with a
remedy for their ills. Being such as we are, to hold
that God made us and then abandoned us would be to
increase a hundredfold the intellectual misery of our situ-

ation. Plato's "great hope" that a God would come and give us "some surer word" than that of human speculation is only the lofty expression of that mute instinct wherewith the whole human race looks upward with agonizing desire for help and for redemption. And help has come, in the fulness of time it came. Dear friends, there is but one institution which can be this manifestation of God in time. If the revelation has not been made already, it will never be made at all. After all these ages of human development, it is useless to expect any other. The heavens will not open again. The race of man has lived on too long, is too far advanced in its manhood and in its sufferings to look for a redeemer yet to come. And there is only one institution which *claims*, absolutely, unflinchingly, and to the uttermost, to be the solution of the difficulties that encompass our existence. Either the Catholic Church is God's agency set in operation and maintained by Him for the salvation of mankind, or else there is no hope from God—nothing but confusion, and struggle, and blind alarm, and ultimate despair.

Thinking men are everywhere seeing this, this solemn alternative; and nowhere are they seeing it more clearly than in this great country of ours, where, by the sweeping away of old forms of thought, intellectual activity has been stimulated into a boldness and accuracy hitherto unknown among the multitude. Nevertheless, there are, unfortunately, many whom this alternative is driving off into the blankness of negation, into the darkness and the cold. And why? Simply because they started in life with a presumption which rules out the claims of the Catholic Church, a presumption instilled into them insensibly from the first opening of their reason—namely, that the old Church has been tried and found wanting; that she was cited at the bar of history and human experience and condemned centuries ago. Of Protestantism as such I cannot stop to speak. It has had its day and is passing, as all human systems of philosophy or religion must surely pass. It was an illogical effort of the human mind to put itself in possession of revelation without the aid of any authority, and all such fallacies are exposed in the end by the inexorable logic of time. But these clear-headed men of whom I speak, though not Protestants themselves, are the descendants of Protestants, and they are suffering from the mistakes of their forefathers; they have inherited what has been well called the Protestant tradition. And they form a large portion, and, let me most willingly say it, some of the best material of this our Republic. To such as these, as well as to my Catholic brethren, I would address myself.

We often say that we are passing through a period of crisis, and that great events are hastening to their solution. The truth is, the world is always in a period of transition and always on the brink of something new. Nevertheless we may safely say it, the present age *is* one of unusual and momentous hesitation. Old things have passed away—what shall be the resultant of the new forces which have already gone into operation? Whether to be or not to be Christian, this is the question which is confronting our modern society; this is the problem which is being silently worked out in many minds, which looms up behind all political quarrels and lies deeper than all social questions or the disputes of capital and labor. Whether to go off into final apostacy, or to cling still to the shreds of hope which flutter towards us from the torn garment of the past. Oh! the choice is a cruel one! and, I believe it, there are many who, not with inward satisfaction but rather with dire anguish, find themselves forced by stress of reason into the abandonment of a creed which once was dear and still seems beautiful.

O, my brethren, look well to it, for the question, the choice is not such as you have supposed. To break utterly with the past, and cast it from us as a thing outworn, is folly, is madness. This is not the true philosophy of evolution. Real development implies continuity. And genuine progress, however swift its march, is not a cutting loose from the past nor a plunging into the darkness. We believe in an evolution more certain and a development more glorious than any which your modern scientists have dreamed of, because we believe that God is infinite activity and that the working out of His plans will bring order out of chaos and lead from darkness into marvellous light.

The problem of the present age is to find some system of thought and action which shall combine perfect stability with limitless progress; and this system is found and can be found only in the Catholic Church. She lays her hand upon the past, with all its treasures of experience, and all that is good in it is hers; she goes forward to meet the future without fear and with unalterable mien, for it also, with all its untold possibilities, shall be hers, to conquer, to inherit and to possess. And she is all this, and can do all this, because she comes from God and because the Divine Wisdom, which "reaches from end to end, directing all things strongly and sweetly," is with her and dwells within her forever. She, the Catholic Church, is the one thing in this world possessed of beauty "ever ancient and ever new;" she is the prudent householder of the Gospel who bringeth from her treasury "things new and old;" she is the bride of the Canticle who sings to her Spouse: "The new and the old, my Beloved, I have kept for Thee;" she is the holy city, the new Jerusalem, "coming down from God out of heaven, prepared as a bride adorned for her husband," and of her is heard the great voice from the throne, saying: "Behold the tabernacle of God with men, and He will dwell with them, and they shall be His people, and God Himself with them shall be their God. And He who sat on the throne said: Behold I make all things new." O loveliest vision! O fairest promise! O sweetest word of God, calling us away from our dull despondency, and bidding us look forward into the freshness of the morning, to the day-dawn of that future when our utmost craving for all that is new and beautiful in the perfection of our race shall be wholly realized!

Lift up your eyes, and look round about, and tell me, my friends, whether you can discern now in this Western World of ours the working of that vitality, that young life constantly renewed, of which I have been speaking.

" Behold I make all things new "—this is the order of
the Divine operation. The old order changes, and yet
God Himself changes not. So it is with His Church.
Her touch transforms, her spirit renews the face of the
earth ; but she herself remains the same. She is always
the same in her character, her mission, her doctrines, her
government ; for these are all of God. But in her dress,
her step and carriage, her mode of dealing with races and
nations, she may vary, for in these things she is capable
of an infinite adaptability.

She proves all things, and holds fast only that which is
good ; she shakes loose and casts from her that which
time has shown to be outworn and worthless ; she per-
petually disencumbers herself, and clad in Divine panoply
stands forth for combat or for suffering. She has waited
in the wilderness, and crouched in the Catacombs ; and
from her throne of honor she has ruled the world with
more than regal sway ; she met the barbarian and curbed
his rage ; she organized a new civilization on the wide
ruin of the old ; she cleared the forest, and drained the
marsh, and built the town ; she covered Europe with her
cathedrals and her colleges ; she was the foster-mother of
learning and the patroness of art ; and all the while she
forgot not that which was ready to perish, but in meek-
ness and voluntary poverty she went her ceaseless rounds
of mercy ; she entered the hovel, the dungeon, the slave-
mart ; she ventured forth, patient and alone, into the
desert and the jungle, through cold and heat, through fire
and martyrdom, pursuing the lost ones of our race even
to the uttermost ends of the earth. All this she has done

in the past, and much more. And now she is here in the midst of us. For a hundred years she has been here, and she is at home in this land. Look upon her, I say, and tell me, what think you of Christ's Church? Whose Spouse is she? Is her form bent and her forehead wrinkled? Are her sandals worn, or her garments moth-eaten? Is her gait halting and feeble, and does she walk with trembling steps? Think you, forsooth, that she is afraid to trust herself to our new civilization? that she clings reluctant to the mouldering fashions of an age that has passed? Oh, see! her face is radiant and her brow erect and starlit, and on her lip is the smile of peace; her robes are beautiful with variety and fragrant as with spices; and the step with which she advances is elastic with triumph. *Vera incessu patuit dea.* Her move-ment betrays her divinity. She is the Daughter of the King.

The work which the Catholic Church has accomplished in this country during the century which we are here bringing to a close is the same which she has done in other ages and in other lands, but she has done it in a new way, and in her own way. She has taken hold of new conditions of things and adapted herself to them; and the result of her work is a structure distinctive and typi-cal of the age and country in which we live, and differing from anything that has preceded it, as truly as the Church of the Middle Ages differed from the Church of the Fa-thers. And mind you—for this is the point of all my dis-course—she has done this, not by any prudence of human forethought, not by any cunning adaptation of policy, but simply because she is a living force, capable of acting in all time and in all places, so that she has become American without ceasing for an instant to be Catholic; and, on the other hand, in endowing us with all that is truly hers, she has not thwarted or crippled, but rather appropriated and vivified all that is best and noblest in our national character.

Therefore, in inaugurating to-day the work of this American Catholic University, we feel that we are the privileged agents of God in carrying on the operations of His Holy Church. If you have read history, however slightly, you know, my friends, that the great universities of Christendom were Catholic in their origin. Long before the outbreak of the sixteenth century, the old cathedral and monastic schools had developed into seats of learning, which dotted every land, until the youth of Europe grew into an army of scholastic enthusiasts. Well, therefore, may we feel that in what we behold accomplished this day, there is nothing forced, or rash, or immature. Surely the time had come for such a work, and surely it was fitting that the Church in America should crown her first century of progress by calling into existence an institution which vindicates once more her claim to an undying vitality. The days of darkness are over; the long winter of poverty and struggle is ended. A brighter era has dawned at last. "Arise, shine, O Jerusalem, for thy light is come, and the glory of the Lord has risen upon thee!"

And now, my friends, before we part, suffer me to bring home to your minds the subject we have been

treating, and to do so in as brief and earnest a manner
as I can. I admit fully that the Church makes no claim
upon your faith which can compel your assent. It is
quite possible to doubt her, to reject her. But are you
justified in rejecting her? Are not the proofs of her
claim sufficient? See, my friend, you believe in God;
but God does not compel your belief. He leaves you
free to deny Him. He does not dazzle and confound
your intelligence by a full manifestation of His glory.
He veils Himself, leaving you proof enough for cer-
tainty, while the very obscurity wherewith He shrouds
Himself makes of your faith a virtue. Now I say that
as surely as there is a God in heaven, just so surely the
Catholic Church is His representative on earth. The
evidence in the one case is as abundant, as convincing
as in the other. And the proof in either case is not
direct; it is cumulative, and let me also add, is over-
whelming.

Jesus Christ has said: "Will ye also go away?"
And again: "Blessed is he whosoever shall not be
scandalized in Me." Wherein lies the secret of this
scandal, this offence? It lies in that very self-same
thing which is the secret of the Church's life and power.
I say it, my friends, with solemn emphasis, the scandal
which turns so many backward is the offence of the
Cross. And it is the Cross of Christ, the preaching of
the Cross, the imitation of the Passion, the life of sacri-
fice, the principle of heroism, which is not merely the
Church's inheritance, but which gives her her glorious
inspiration and constitutes her undying force. Outside

of the Catholic Church the doctrine of the Cross has
faded into a vague tradition. There are many who pro-
fess to believe in the Son of God, but the mystery of His
Cross and Passion has become for them a sentimental
abstraction or a cold philosophy. Oh that those whose
hearts can still be stirred by the contemplation of the
most wondrous tragedy the world has ever witnessed
might come to learn that there exists on earth a kingdom of souls in which Jesus Christ is loved, and
worshipped, and imitated with a passionate devotion
unknown to them in their forlorn isolation! The life
of Christ is the life of His Church, but it is a life pur-
chased by suffering and death. He is risen, and is with
her still; and as He died and rose again, so she dies
with Him continually, and rises into a life new and
immortal. See! in this nineteenth century she has risen
again before your very eyes! Death hath no more
dominion over her.

————————

II.

THE BANQUET.

The morning solemnities ended shortly after one o'clock. All were then invited to partake of the refreshments abundantly provided for them. In the Banquet Hall, beneath the Chapel, dinner was served for two hundred and fifty guests, while, in the Refectory, company after company, to the number of about fourteen hundred, found hearty welcome and plenteous entertainment. This was all that was physically possible, and showed at least the desire of the University to provide without stint for the comfort of its honored visitors.

The principal feature in the adornment of the Banquet Hall were large ornamental shields bearing the names of the chief universities of the world, with their motto and the date of their institution. The flags of the various countries in which the universities are located festooned the walls and ceiling. Life-sized portraits of Cardinals Gibbons, McCloskey, Manning, Newman and Wiseman, and Father Faber, looked down upon the scene, a likeness of our Holy Father the Pope presiding over all. With the Cardinals, Archbishops, Bishops, Prelates, Vicars General, heads of Religious

Orders and presidents of educational institutions, were
mingled distinguished representatives of the civil government and the chief benefactors of the University.
As at the laying of the corner-stone, so also on this
memorable occasion, the President and Vice-President
of the United States, together with several members of
the Cabinet, showed by their presence the deep interest
felt in the new institution by the whole people of our
country. Some distinguished representatives of the
South American States, then in Washington for the
Pan-American Congress, were also present to show
the sympathy of their countries in the great undertaking.

Towards the close of the dinner, the toasts were pro-
posed. The first of these was "OUR HOLY FATHER,
POPE LEO XIII." It was responded to by the Holy
Father's representative, the Most Rev. Monsignor
Satolli. With the Ciceronian eloquence for which he
is so renowned, he discoursed in Latin of classical
beauty on the paternal love of our great Pope for
America and her free institutions, and on the special
interest and the heartfelt joy, with which he regarded
the inauguration of this home of highest learning in
the midst of our western Republic. He showed how,
in all ages, the highest advances of Christian civilization have been marked by the glories of the great
universities. And in order that the civilization of our
country, by being truly Christian, might be truly salu-
tary to herself and to the nations of the earth, on whom
she exercises so great an influence, it was, he said, the

wish and the prayer of our Holy Father that the union of the highest sacred learning with the fullest natural science, of which this institution was meant to be the embodiment, should be a beacon-light to point out to our country the safe paths, should be a leaven of truth and grace to the minds and hearts of all our people.

His eloquent utterances, so full of love for learning and love for religion, of devotedness to the Holy Father and admiration for America, to whom, as he said, the Pope believed that all things were possible, were received by the distinguished audience with enthusiastic applause.

Just as Monsignor Satolli was concluding, a cablegram was received from the Rev. Dr. Farrelly of the American College in Rome, announcing that the Holy Father sent his congratulations and special benediction. Nothing could have been more opportune than this delightful incident. It is needless to say that this fresh testimony of the Holy Father's interest and affection was welcomed with unbounded enthusiasm.

To the second toast, "OUR COUNTRY AND HER PRESIDENT," a graceful reply was made by the Hon. James G. Blaine, Secretary of State. He dwelt upon the impartiality of the American government in dealing with all forms of religion, fully securing the rights and liberties of each by the guarantees surrounding the rights and liberties of all. He spoke of America's reverence for learning and for religion, both necessary conditions for her sure and safe progress, and was glad to pay honor to an institution aiming at the cultivation of both.

At this juncture, President Harrison himself entered, the band playing " Hail to the Chief," and was received with great applause, which he acknowledged in a few pleasant words of thanks.

The third toast was, " OUR SISTER UNIVERSITIES." It was most fittingly responded to by the Cardinal Archbishop of Quebec, formerly Rector and now Chancellor of the Laval University, and the only surviving signer of its act of incorporation. Speaking in French, for the sake of greater fluency, he dwelt with becoming pride on the deep interest which the Catholics of Canada had always manifested in the cause of Christian education, and the noble work they had accomplished for its extension and improvement. He noted the elevating influence exercised upon the whole educational system by a great central institution like Laval. He alluded in friendly tones to the offshoots of the old Alma Mater now appearing in Montreal and Ottawa. He spoke of the interest with which Canada had regarded the institutions of higher learning hitherto founded in the United States, of which respectful and affectionate mention had been made in introducing the toast; and he augured fullest success and glory for this new and crowning work of the system of Christian education in our country.

In responding to the next toast: " THE HIERARCHY OF THE UNITED STATES," the Cardinal Archbishop of Baltimore, after thanking the President of the United States, the Vice-President and the members of the Cabinet, for their distinguished presence, said: " It is a subject of profound satisfaction and of deep significance to witness so many of the American Episcopate present on this festive occasion. They have come from nearly every State and Territory of the Union ; from the shores of the Atlantic and the Pacific, and from the banks of the St. Lawrence and the Mississippi.

They have come, not in compliance with any law or obligation, but in obedience to the promptings of their own generous hearts. And by assisting to-day at these dedicatory exercises, they eloquently proclaim their warm interest in this great seat of learning, and they emphasize the fact that this Institution is not a work of merely local significance, but is invested with national importance. And by participating in these festivities at great inconvenience to themselves, they emphasize another fact,— that, as the Catholic University of America had its origin in the deliberations of the Bishops in Council assembled, so are the Bishops prepared to stand its sponsors, and for all time to come it is to be under the fatherly control and supervision of the American Episcopate.

When I speak of the Hierarchy, I desire of course to associate with them the Clergy, without whose aid the Bishops would be practically powerless, and by whose generous coöperation the success of this great undertaking will be assured.

When I contemplate these stately buildings, and the sacred purposes to which they are consecrated; when I look around me and behold this large and enthusiastic assemblage, the earnest and the first-fruits of the students who are to follow, the sublime words of the Prophet Isaias come to my mind, and I reverently and confidently

accept them as a prophecy for us : " Arise, be enlightened,
O Jerusalem, for thy light is come, and the glory of the
Lord is risen upon thee; the Gentiles shall walk in thy
light, and Kings in the brightness of thy rising. Lift up
thy eyes round about and see. All these are gathered
together. They are come to thee. *Thy sons shall come
from afar.*" Yes, the sons of the sovereign people shall
come hither, to receive intellectual light and strength and
that wisdom which is born of God; and they will go
forth from these walls to enlighten their country by
their knowledge, to enrich it by their wisdom, to edify
it by their example, and if needs be, to defend it by
their valor."

His Eminence then called upon the Most Rev. P. J.
Ryan, Archbishop of Philadelphia, who, in an address
sparkling with wit and eloquence, sketched the character-
istics of the leaders of the Hierarchy there present, to
the great enjoyment of all the company.

The final toast was: " THE PRESS, THE GREAT CO-
EDUCATOR OF THE WORLD." Mr. John Boyle O'Reilly,
editor of the Boston Pilot, gracefully responded in the
following poem :

FROM THE HEIGHTS.

" COME to me for wisdom," said the mountain ;
" In the valley and the plain
  There is knowledge dimmed with sorrow in the gain ;
  There is Effort, with its hope like a fountain ;
  There, the chainèd rebel, Passion,
  Laboring Strength and fleeting Fashion ;

There, Ambition's leaping flame,
And the iris-crown of Fame.
But those gains are dear forever
Won from loss and pain and fever.
Nature's gospel never changes;
Every sudden force deranges;
Blind endeavor is not wise:
Wisdom enters through the eyes;
And the seer is the knower,
Is the doer and the sower.

"Come to me for riches," said the peak;
"I am leafless, cold and calm;
But the treasures of the lily and the palm—
They are mine to bestow on those who seek.
I am gift and I am giver
To the verdured fields below,
As the motherhood of snow
Daily gives the new-born river.
As a watcher on a tower,
Listening to the evening hour,
Sees the roads diverge and blend,
Sees the wandering currents end
Where the moveless waters shine
On the far horizon line—
All the storied Past is mine;
All its strange beliefs still clinging;
All its singers and their singing;
All the paths that led astray,
All the meteors once called day;
All the stars that rose to shine—
Come to me—for all are mine!

" Come to me for safety," said the height ;
" In the future as the past,
  Road and river end at last
  In the bosom of the ever-waiting sea.
  Who shall know by lessened sight
  Where the gain and where the loss
  In the desert they must cross ?
  Guides who lead their charge from ills,
  Passing soon from town to town,
  Through the forest and the down,
  Take direction from the hills ;
  Those who range a wider land
  Higher climb until they stand
  Where the past and future swing
  Round them like an ocean-ring ;
  Those who sail from land afar
  Leap from mountain-top to star.
  Higher still, from star to God,
  Have the spirit-pilots trod,
  Setting lights for mind and soul
  That the ships may reach their goal.

" They shall safely steer who see :
  Sight is wisdom.   Come to me !"

III

THE PRESENTATIONS.

From the Banquet Hall the company repaired to the parlors, for the next part of the day's programme; and in an instant, the large parlor, the smaller reception rooms, and the spacious hallway between them, were filled with a multitude eager to witness the presentation of the bust of St. Thomas Aquinas, and the addresses from the great educational centres abroad.

PRESENTATION OF THE BUST OF ST. THOMAS.

The immediate object of general interest was the splendid bust of the Angelic Doctor, looking down with serene majesty on the group which instinctively gathered around it. The Catholics of Great Britain and Ireland, residing in Rome, anxious to manifest their interest in a work which had grown familiar to every English-speaking Catholic in the Eternal City, had rightly judged that the most appropriate and welcome testimonial that they could offer would be a marble bust of the Angel of the Schools. The well-known effigy

39

of the Saint, on the Pincian Hill, was at first considered
the best model to reproduce. But Guglielmi, the celebrated Roman sculptor, to whom they entrusted the task,
decided that something better still could be produced.
For that purpose he studied the portraits of St. Thomas,
in various parts of Italy, which were considered the most
authentic; and the result is this superb work, which
may well be considered the best likeness of the Angelic
Doctor in existence. On the marble pedestal is the
following inscription, by the renowned Roman Latinist,
Father Angelini, S. J.:

LYCEO · MAGNO

WASHINGTONII

IN · REGIONIBUS · FOEDERATIS

AMERICAE · BOREALIS

AUSPICIIS · LEONIS · $\overline{\text{XIII}}$ · P · M ·

CONSTITUTO

THOMAE · AQUINATIS

STUDIORUM

DUCIS · ET · MAGISTRI

SIGNUM

GRATULATIONIS · ET · AMORIS

PIGNUS

DONO · DANT

ANGLI · SCOTI · HIBERNI

ROMAM . INCOLENTES

A · $\overline{\text{MDCCCLXXXIX}}$

ANTONIUS ANGELINIUS

E SOCIETATE JESU

The Rt. Rev. John Virtue, Bishop of Portsmouth, and the Very Rev. Monsignor C. J. Gadd, of the Diocese of Salford, in the name of the donors, made the presentation. Monsignor Gadd read the following address, a beautifully illuminated copy of which he handed to the Rector.

To the Right Reverend Bishop Keane, Rector of the Catholic University of Washington.

My Lord Bishop :—

In presenting, on behalf of the Catholics of Great Britain and Ireland in Rome, this marble Bust of Saint Thomas Aquinas to the Catholic University of Washington, through your Lordship, its first Rector, we, the members of the Presentation Committee, desire to express the deep interest which we feel in your great undertaking, and our most ardent wishes for its success.

The privileges granted to the new University by the Holy See are a fresh proof of the paternal charity and wisdom of the Sovereign Pontiffs, who, in desiring the conversion of all men to the true Faith, have endeavored also to provide them with a solid and enlightened education —an education including all the cultivation of which the human mind is capable, in philosophy, theology, science, literature, and art. Such was the education introduced into England by Saint Gregory the Great, who sent Saint Augustine to preach the Gospel to the English people; it had been introduced 170 years before among the Irish and Scotch, by Saint Celestine; and the same stream of Christian learning, ever flowing from its infallible source, has continued to this day, and has now brought to the United States of America the Catholic University of Washington, which is destined to fill a great place in the history of the English-speaking races throughout the world.

But, besides the expression of our deep interest and ardent wishes, we desire by this presentation to draw closer, under the glorious patronage of the Angelic Doctor Saint Thomas, the links which already bind us together, so that we, who are members of the same Christian family, and of kindred blood, may become more and more united in faith, hope, and charity.

With this pledge of our brotherly love, we offer to your Lordship our heartfelt congratulations on the Centenary of the Foundation of your noble Episcopate, which, springing from a single See, overshadows at this day with its Pastoral care your vast Commonwealth.

The sentiments which we have briefly expressed are, we do not doubt, abundantly shared by your Lordship; and we feel sure that, in accepting our humble offering, your Lordship and the University will look less to its intrinsic value than to the spirit of Catholic unity of which it is a proof.

We are, my Lord Bishop,
With profound respect,
Your Lordship's faithful and devoted servants,

✠ TOBIAS KIRBY, *Archbishop of Ephesus.*
✠ EDMUND STONOR, *Archbishop of Trebizond.*
JAMES A. CAMPBELL, *Rector of the Scots' College.*
WILLIAM GILES, *Rector of the English College.*

we, who are members of the same
and of kindred blood, may become more
in faith, hope, and charity.
ge of our brotherly love, we offer to your
artfelt congratulations on the Centenary
ion of your noble Episcopate, which,
single See, overshadows at this day with
your vast Commonwealth.

which we have briefly expressed are,
abundantly shared by your Lordship:
hat, in accepting our humble offering,
d the University will look less to its
.. to the spirit of Catholic unity of

From the time that the first step was taken towards
establishment of the Catholic University of America,
most friendly interest in the undertaking has been ma
fested by the Catholic Universities of France. This v
shown on the present occasion by the addresses sent
the Universities of Paris and Lyons. In the followi
letter Mgr. d'Hulst, Rector of the Catholic University
Paris, and a fast friend of our University from the beg
ning, expressed his regret at not being able to assist
the inauguration himself, and introduced the Visco
de Meaux, who was to represent both Paris and Lyo

INSTITUT CATHOLIQUE DE PARIS.

74, RUE DE V......

devoir rigoureux me retenait donc. Dans cette conjoncture c'est un vrai bonheur pour moi, pour nous tous, de trouver dans la personne de Mr. le Vicomte de Meaux, ancien ministre, gendre de notre grand Montalembert, un représentant qui consent à porter nos vœux et nos cordiales salutations aux fondateurs de l'Université d'Amerique.

Ecrivain distingué, auteur d'ouvrages historiques importants sur la Réforme protestante en France, Mr. de Meaux est digne par son talent et par l'ardeur de sa foi de continuer les glorieuses traditions de sa famille.

Je suis heureux de remettre entre ses mains l'addresse de notre Université à la votre. Je regrette seulement que la signature d'un bon nombre de nos professeurs, qui ne sont pas encore rentrés, manque au bas de cette pièce. Tous ceux qui sont à Paris l'ont signée avec joie et s'unissent à moi pour vous exprimer les sentiments fraternels qui nous animent envers votre personne et votre œuvre.

Plus libres que nous, vous pourrez mieux faire. Que Dieu bénisse vos efforts! Tous vos succès trouveront dans nos cœurs un joyeux écho.

Je me permets de recommander à votre plus bienveillant accueil notre éminent délégué et je le charge de renouveler particulièrement en mon nom à Votre Grandeur l'hommage des sentiments respectueux avec lesquels j'ai l'honneur d'être, Monseigneur,

Votre dévoué et reconnaissant serviteur,

M. D'HULST,

V. G., Recteur.

ur,
as
ly

Messieurs, l'est encore aujourd'hui ; toujours disposée à répandre au dehors ce qu'elle sait, ce qu'elle pense et ce qu'elle croit, elle est restée, dans la vieille Europe, le premier peuple missionnaire. C'est le témoignage que lui a rendu l'homme dont la parole est votre lumière, votre force et votre gloire.

Eminence, avant de venir dans votre pays, j'avais lu, avec une émotion reconnaissante, ce que vous avez écrit sur le mien au lendemain de ses revers, et je me félicite particulièrement de pouvoir, ici, en ce moment, vous en rendre grâces. A mon tour, lorsque j'aurai repassé l'Atlantique, j'essayerai de représenter à mes compatriotes ce que je vois en ce moment, un grand peuple et une grande Eglise, l'un et l'autre contents et confiants, contents du présent, confiants dans l'avenir.

Je leur dirai que chez ce peuple, destiné à mêler ensemble toutes les races du monde, en les rajeunissant dans un bain de vie et de liberté, chez ce peuple libre, j'ai vu l'Eglise vraiment libre, j'ai vu la liberté servir au progrès de la religion et la religion concourir au maintien de la liberté. Je leur dirai encore que, chez ce peuple, où le travail, plus actif et plus fécond qu'il n'a jamais été sur la terre, enfante, accroît, accumule la richesse, j'ai vu cette richesse mise au service de la religion et de la science, consacrée au développement de l'esprit humain sous l'égide de la foi chrétienne.

C'est le spectacle que donne en naissant l'Université Catholique de Washington ; l'avenir qui lui est promis lui attire, dès ce jour, un fraternel hommage de ses sœurs de Paris et de Lyon.

He then presented the following addresses:

PARIS, *le 23 Octobre, 1889.*

A Son Eminence le CARDINAL GIBBONS,

A NN. SS. les ARCHEVÊQUES et EVÊQUES des Etats-
Unis d'Amerique.

A Monseigneur le RECTEUR,
Et à tous les membres du corps professoral de l'Université Catholique de Washington.

Eminence,
Messeigneurs,
Messieurs,

L'Université Catholique de Paris, née il y a quinze ans,
envoie, en vos personnes, à la naissante Université Catholique de Washington, ses vœux fraternels et l'expression
de ses plus cordiales sympathies.

Dans le Nouveau comme dans l'Ancien Monde, l'hu-
manité s'agite à la recherche de la Science et perd le
souci de la vérité. Il appartient aux enfants de la véri-
table Eglise de faire cesser ce divorce entre les faits et
les principes. Pour cela ils doivent entrer résolûment
dans le champ de la Science, y apporter un esprit hardi
et sincère, mais y faire pénétrer avec eux la lumière
des vérités supérieures dont ils ont la garde.

Les Universités seront les foyers de cette science
à la fois ancienne et nouvelle, qui, par le respect des
traditions et l'ardeur des recherches, doit relier le passé
à l'avenir.

Salut à nos frères d'Amérique qui entreprennent de mettre la puissance de leur initiative et les ressources d'une vraie liberté au service de la foi dans les hautes régions du savoir!

D'un bord à l'autre de l'Océan, l'affection, l'estime, l'émulation de vos frères d'Europe vont au-devant de vos efforts et de vos espérances.

Le 13 Novembre prochain, tandis que nous tiendrons à Paris notre Séance annuelle de rentrée, sous la présidence des trente-deux Evêques fondateurs de notre Institut, nous serons aussi présents de cœur à Washington pour l'inauguration de votre Université,

Quam Deus sospitet, augeat et ornet!

M. D'HULST, *prélat domestique de S. S.*
recteur de l'Université Catholique de Paris.

[Signed also by the Professors of the various Faculties.]

A L'UNIVERSITÉ CATHOLIQUE D'AMÉRIQUE
L'UNIVERSITÉ CATHOLIQUE DE LYON.

C'est avec un tressaillement d'allégresse que nous avons reçu de Son Eminence le cardinal Gibbons et de Sa Grandeur Monseigneur Keane, l'honorable message qui nous conviait à votre inauguration. L'un de nos amis, fils de l'Eglise de Lyon, M. le Vicomte de Meaux, gendre de l'illustre Comte de Montalembert, le glorieux champion de la liberté de l'enseignement, veut bien se charger de nous représenter auprès de vous. Il vous portera nos félicitations et nos vœux.

Nous saluons dans votre naissance l'un des plus heureux événements de ce siècle, l'un des plus glorieux pour l'Eglise romaine et son auguste Chef.

N'êtes vous pas un nouveau gage de la haute et incessante sollicitude de Léon XIII pour le progrès des Lettres et des Sciences chrétiennes, qu'une cruelle oppression ne peut lui faire oublier?

Vous êtes la preuve vivante de la fécondité de l'Eglise, notre mère, qui, en si peu de temps, a enfanté tant de merveilles parmi vous.

Vous nous donnez le salutaire exemple de l'accord qui doit régner entre l'Eglise et la vraie liberté. Nous vous regardons d'un œil d'envie, et nous soupirons après le jour où notre vieille Europe, prenant modèle sur la jeune Amérique, reconnaîtra que la liberté n'a pas de meilleure amie ni de plus sûre garantie que la religion de Celui qui l'a apportée au monde et l'a arrosée de son divin sang.

Puisse le jeune arbre que l'Eglise vient de planter sur votre sol généreux croître et se développer! Qu'il se couvre promptement de fruits! Que les Etats-Unis, que toute l'Amérique en profitent, et que notre foi en reçoive un nouveau lustre dans l'univers entier! Que l'ancien et le nouveau monde, unis dans la même foi et le même amour, travaillent de concert à la gloire de Dieu et à l'extension de son règne sur la terre!

Tels sont les vœux fraternels que l'Université catholi-

50

que de Lyon forme pour sa jeune sœur d'Amérique ;
daigne la divine bonté les exaucer !

☠ JOSEPH, CARD. FOULON, *Archev. de Lyon,*
Chancelier de l' Université Catholique de Lyon.

J. CARRAY, *Prélat de la maison de S.S.*
Recteur de l' Université.

[Signed also by all the Professors in the Faculties of Theology, Law,
Letters and Sciences.]

On the very day of our inauguration, there was held in
Paris a meeting of the Prelates under whose patronage
the Catholic University of that city is conducted. They
were not unmindful of the kindred work then being com-
menced in the western world, and testified their friendly
sympathy in the following telegram :

PARIS, *le 13 Novembre, 1889.*

"Cardinaux, Archevêques, Evêques, réunis à Paris
pour Conseil de l'Université Catholique, envoient aux
Evêques américains vœux fraternels pour l'Université de
Washington."

Signed : CARDINAL BERNADOU, *Archevêque de Sens.*
CARDINAL RICHARD, *Archevêque de Paris.*

THE LAVAL UNIVERSITY.

The Laval University of Quebec was not only represented by the Cardinal Archbishop, its Chancellor, but
also by its excellent Rector, the Rt. Rev. Mgr. Benj.
Paquet. The latter, in his robes of office, made an address expressive of the sisterly gladness and love with
which the Laval University welcomed the Catholic University of America into the realms of higher education in
which she had herself so long reigned with honor; and
as a pledge of the links of affection which were forever,
he trusted, to unite the two institutions in the same
noble and holy work, he, in the name of his University,
bestowed on the Rector of the new University the degree
and diploma of Doctor of Divinity.

THE UNIVERSITY OF OTTAWA.

The University of Ottawa, which, from the rank of
College, had reached the dignity of a University within
the last few months, was also represented by its Chancellor, the Most Rev. Joseph T. Duhamel, Archbishop of
Ottawa, and by its President, the Very Rev. Celestin
Augier, who, immediately after the address of Mgr.
Paquet, gave utterance to similar sentiments in the name
of his University. The fact that the Providence of God
had called these two seats of learning into existence at

the same time, should be a lasting guarantee, he said, of their mutual attachment, and an additional incentive to holy rivalry in doing great work for God and for country.

THE UNIVERSITY OF LOUVAIN.

The venerable University of Louvain, which all the Catholic Universities of the world revere and look to as a model, was not able to send a representative to the inauguration, though its officials had repeatedly expressed the desire that it might be in their power to do so. But the Rector Magnificus, the Rt. Rev. Mgr. Abbeloos, expressed the sentiments of the entire Faculty in the following telegram:

"LOUVAIN, *Nov. 12th, 1889.*

The University of Louvain rejoices at the glorious celebration of the American Centennial by the founding of the Catholic University. Glory to God! Happiness to the American people."

Signed: "RECTOR ABBELOOS."

This was followed by a letter from the Rt. Rev. Mgr. Mercier, the distinguished Professor of Higher Philosophy at Louvain, breathing in warmest words the fraternal sympathy with which he has watched and aided the work from its commencement.

THE AMERICAN COLLEGE AT ROME.

Besides the telegram of the Rev. Dr. Farrelly, conveying the congratulations and blessing of the Holy Father, the American College at Rome sent another dispatch in the name of all its students. During the months which, on two occasions, the Rector had spent there, attending to the business of the University with the Holy See, our American students in the Eternal City had in very many ways manifested the profound interest with which they watched every stage of its development. And now that the day had come for its being launched forth to its work, they sent a joint message of rejoicing and of loving good wishes, signed by the worthy Vice Rector of the College, presiding in the absence of Mgr. O'Connell, who was present with us, in their name and in his own.

ST. MARY'S, OSCOTT.

A beautifully illuminated address was sent by the Bishop of Birmingham, signed by himself, as Rector of the Seminary of St. Mary's, Oscott, and by all the Faculty of that historic institution. It ran as follows:

"To the Right Rev. John J. Keane, Bishop of Ajasso, Rector of the Catholic University, Washington.

"We, the Rector, Professors, and Students of the Birmingham Diocesan Seminary, at St. Mary's, Oscott, hasten to offer our warm congratulations on the auspicious day of the opening of the new American University. For the establishment of a Catholic University in the New World, after long forethought, with such suitability to the needs of the age, and with large-minded and characteristic generosity, is an event to gladden the hearts of Catholics throughout the world.

" The foreshadowing and growth of your ideal we have watched with a lively and fraternal interest; and for the day of solemn inauguration we send you our cordial greetings, that you may know we are rejoicing with you, and praying that the noble conception of the great Hierarchy of the States may grow with the growth of your people, and may prosper and be blessed, like those historic universities of our Old World, and never fail, as some have done, in the glory of their submission to the Church of Christ.

" We have, moreover, to present to your Lordship our hearty congratulations on your appointment to the distinguished and responsible office of First Rector, and on the conspicuous success of your labors.

" And lastly, we desire to greet with sincere affection the Staff you have gathered around you, in whom we all recognize men of worth and ability, and some of us our personal friends."

(The Signatures.)

November 2d, 1889.

ST. CUTHBERT'S, USHAW.

From the President and Faculty of St. Cuthbert's College, Ushaw, Durham, the following address was received, through the Very Rev. Monsignor Gadd.

" *My Dear Lord:*

" On occasion of the solemn inauguration of the Catholic University at Washington, I desire to convey to your Lordship, in the name of my fellow-Professors and my own, our warmest congratulations and heartfelt joy.

" For more than a quarter of a century, the establishment of a Catholic University has occupied the minds of their Lordships, the Bishops of the United States. For they felt that the intellectual needs of their country could only be adequately met by a seat of the highest learning, a nursery of literature, art, and science, similar to those which have been the glory of the Catholic Church in every age and country. By the inauguration of the Catholic University in the Metropolis of America, their ardent wishes are now to be realized and this long-felt want supplied. It is hardly possible to overrate the importance of this noble and glorious work, stamped as it is with the seal of our Holy Father, Pope Leo XIII, and destined, under the blessing of God and His Vicar, to bring forth fruits of inestimable value both to the Church and country of America.

May the young men of America be impressed with a laudable ambition of profiting by the advantages now offered them ; may they be led gladly to enter a sanctuary, from which the light of true doctrine will radiate, and where education will be the handmaid of Religion.

Allow us then to join with the rest of the Christian world in congratulating you on this memorable day, and in wishing success to the great work you are inaugurating. It is our earnest and heartfelt prayer that God may bless and prosper this work, and that He may preserve your Lordship in health and strength for many a year, to encourage and guide the youth of the Catholic University of Washington in the paths of virtue and learning.

With kindest regards, and renewed good wishes,

Believe me, my dear Lord,

Your obedient and faithful servant,

JAMES LEMON,
President.

Nov. 3d, 1889.

ST. BEDE'S COLLEGE, MANCHESTER.

From the above-named institution, one of the monuments of Bishop Vaughan's zeal for Christian education, came the following address, also through the courtesy of Monsignor Gadd. It is inscribed in a beautiful album of photographic views of the College.

" To THE RIGHT REV. JOHN J. KEANE, BISHOP OF JASSUS, RECTOR OF THE CATHOLIC UNIVERSITY, WASHINGTON.

"The Rector, Professors, and Students of St. Bede's College, Manchester, take advantage of the happy circumstance of the presence of their Vice-Rector at the Inauguration of the Catholic University of America, to respectfully present to your Lordship their sincere congratulations upon this most auspicious event in the history of the Catholic Church in the United States of North America.

" The erection of the Catholic University is the glorious crowning of the marvellous record of progress and development which, under the blessing of Divine Providence, has unrolled itself during the brief course of a century in the great Republic connected by the triple bond of blood and speech and Faith with the Catholics of these islands. Nothing that affects the welfare of the Church in the United States can be indifferent to the Church in this land. But the great question of Catholic Education, the most vital question affecting the Church of the present day, is above all the one which most deeply stirs the sympathy and interest of all those who are in any way practically engaged in it. In thus completing the noble edifice, by the erection of the supreme Academical Institution of a great National Alma Mater, the Catholics of the United States are setting a splendid example, which we in England at present may only admire at a distance, but which we may fondly hope some day to imitate.

"A Catholic College like ours, which is entirely devoted to the work of modern and commercial education, may claim a special right to watch with deep and sympathetic interest the Catholic educational work of a great country, so eminent amongst the nations for its progressive spirit, the vigor of its energy and enterprise, the fertility of its inventive resource, and above all for that frank and unreserved liberty, under which the Church is left free to expand her energies and devote the fulness of her strength to the healing and helping of peoples."

Signed,   "THOMAS CANON WRENNALL,

Rector."

[Signed also by the entire Faculty, and by a committee of the students in the name of the rest.]

THE ARCHBISHOPS AND BISHOPS OF GREAT BRITAIN AND IRELAND.

Besides the messages of fraternal greeting sent directly to the University, precious words concerning its establishment were embodied in the addresses sent by the Archbishops and Bishops of Great Britain and Ireland on the occasion of the Centenary of our Hierarchy.

The Archbishops of Armagh, Dublin, Cashel, and Tuam, in the name of all the Irish Prelates, write as follows:

"To the great Thanksgiving with which you close the hundred years just passed, you are to add, Venerable

Brethren, another scarcely less illustrious act with which
to open the second century of the American Church.
The Catholic University of America is, indeed, a mighty
name to write upon the first page of the new record. It
is an achievement and a promise. It is the fruit of the
steady growth of Catholic Education in the United States
for the last hundred years; and it contains the seeds of
yet greater development in the time to come. We have
learned too well in Ireland what it is to be without a
Catholic University equal to our needs. Year after year
have we deplored the disabilities that either deprived
our Catholic youth of higher education altogether, or
drove them, in their search for it, whither our blessing
could not follow them. From our inmost hearts, therefore, we felicitate you on the glorious inauguration of
your Catholic University; and we pray that the blessing
of LEO which speeds it on its way, may guard it through
ages yet to come, to be a guiding light to the great intellect of America, and the nursing Mother of those whose
wisdom and whose sanctity will instruct her noble people
unto justice."

In the joint address of the Bishops of Hexam and
Newcastle, Leeds, Salford, Liverpool, Middlesbrough, and .
Shrewsbury, the establishment of the Catholic University is thus beautifully dwelt upon:
"Above all, we are impressed with your zeal for a
higher education. We have heard with singular interest
of the determination of the American Hierarchy to crown

their system of Catholic schools and colleges by the erection of a Catholic University. Living as we do in the midst of a world which is agitated by intellectual strife, we feel the extreme importance to Catholics of a course of such higher studies as are proper to a University; while at the same time we are profoundly convinced that a Catholic spirit and a Catholic atmosphere are as essential for the training and formation of Catholic youth during the University period of their education as excellence in method and brilliancy in teaching power.

"You have been unwilling to compromise the future of the Catholic Church in America by attaching your Catholic youth to any of your great national seats of learning, because you knew that these, not being frankly Catholic, would never be places of education for Catholic youth. You have not hesitated, therefore, during the infancy of your Church, to lay the foundations of a purely Catholic University, which shall develop and expand with your growth during centuries to come.

"We congratulate you upon the lofty ideal, the public spirit, the splendid generosity, which you have found in your Catholic people, and upon the wisdom which has induced you, with the consent and coöperation of all, to begin by founding that portion of a University curriculum, which is made up of the various branches of sacred science. For while Religion must always be the foundation of a University education, there seems to be a special reason why higher education in your University should begin with the Clergy. The Priesthood is designed by God to be the salt of the earth and the guardian of truth.

It would therefore appear to be a matter of the highest prudence and forethought, in considering the common weal, to make special and early provision for the education of a succession of highly-trained Ecclesiastics, whose lives may become consecrated to learning and to the elucidation of truth. They, as a class, will become the most useful servants of the Republic, because they will, as skilled and well-trained men of science, deal with those errors which are ever attacking the fundamental truths of philosophy and revelation, and endeavoring to turn the world back to that worship of nature which Christ our Lord, the Saviour of the World, came to destroy and to supplant.

"We, therefore, congratulate your Eminence, and our brethren of the great American Hierarchy, upon the celebration of the Centenary of the Church of the United States, and we wish you God-speed in the noble undertaking in behalf of truth and learning on which you are engaged. May it become a worthy memorial of a Catholic people's gratitude to God for the Divine Goodness which has abundantly blessed them during the century which has just closed; may it become the matrix of their intellectual strength, the arsenal of natural science and Divine Truth, and a beacon, shining brightly over your land, of fidelity and obedience to Blessed Peter and to his Holy Roman See."

IV

THE FORMAL OPENING OF THE COURSES.

Shortly after 4 o'clock, the strains of the Marine Band playing a national anthem summoned all to the Lecture Hall, for the exercises which were to formally inaugurate the University courses of instruction. Every inch of the stage and of the auditorium was filled with the assemblage of Prelates, Clergy, and laity, while thousands filled all the space around, whence even a distant glimpse of the scene could be obtained.

After the chanting of the *Veni Sancte Spiritus*, his Eminence, Cardinal Gibbons, offered up the prayer to the Holy Ghost.

The Rt. Rev. M. J. O'Farrell, Bishop of Trenton, then delivered the inaugural oration. In language whose eloquence called forth frequent rounds of hearty applause, he showed the relation between Divine Truth and human science, and sketched the action of the Church in all ages as the faithful expounder of the one and the generous patron of the other. Having demonstrated that, in the nature of things, there can be no contradiction between God's word and God's works, that it is absurd to suppose a thing true in theology and false in science, or the reverse, he put in admirably clear light the consequence that religion cannot possibly have anything to fear from the advance of scientific discovery, nor scientific progress any reason to look with dread or disfavor upon fidelity to religious convictions. Then glancing down the history of education and of intellectual advancement in all countries, he showed that, in fact, science never obtained greater successes than in times and countries distinctively Catholic; that in the most remarkable intellects that have ever existed, clearness and strength of faith was usually associated with a reverent eagerness to search out the ways of God in creation, for the Creator's glory and for the utility of human life; that the Church's word of caution against rashness of assertion was never meant as a hindrance to real discovery; that Popes and Prelates most distinguished for zeal for the faith have ordinarily been foremost advocates and patrons of literature, art, and science. Finally, he dwelt upon the spectacle, now attracting the admiration of the world, of our country, foremost in industrial energy, in inventive genius, in social progress, in intellectual eagerness; and yet presenting statistics of the Church's advancement such as can hardly elsewhere be equalled. The establishment in the heart of such a country of an institution aiming at the perfect union of religion and science, was, he argued, a significant summing up of all the history of past ages, and a splendid augury of the mingled light of divine and human truth which was safely to guide our new world in still nobler paths for the future.

It is greatly to be regretted that circumstances have hindered the learned Prelate from writing in full, for publication, the admirable discourse of which the above is too meagre an outline. Its merit is all the greater because of the circumstances under which it was delivered. The Inaugural Oration was to have been given by the Rt. Rev. J. L. Spalding, Bishop of Peoria. When assailed by ill health, he sent timely warning; but the hope was still entertained, till within a few days of the Inauguration, that he might yet be able to fulfil his engagement. It was when it became certain, almost at the last moment, that he could not come, that the Bishop of Trenton generously consented to make the effort, which succeeded so admirably.

After a few moments of intermission, enlivened by the music of the Band, the Very Rev. Monsignor Joseph Schroeder, D. D., Professor of Dogmatic Theology and Dean of the Present Faculty of the University, spoke as follows:

Eminentissimi Principes,
Illustrissimi ac Reverendissimi Praesules,
Auditores Colendissimi, Ornatissimi,

SI viros summa praeditos eloquentia, cum ad dicendum venissent, sive loci amplitudine, sive audientium dignitate, immo etiam unius principis adspectu ita conturbatos fuisse accepimus, ut pro magna sua moderatione atque modestia silentium sibi imperarent, quo tandem animo ego affectus sim oportet, qui tum virium mearum tenuitatem ingeniique mediocritatem apprime sentiam, tum in ea dicendi conditione sim constitutus, ut quae singula oratorum animos commovere consueverint, ea mihi sese hodierno die offerant atque obiiciant universa? Non enim in unum tantum principem oculorum aciem converto, sed quotquot sanctae ecclesiae pastores, quotquot nobilissimae huius reipublicae firmamenta, quotquot ornamenta virtutum, artium scientiarumque lumina conspicio, totidem mihi consessum principum videor intueri! Accedit quod adstante lectissimorum hominum frequentia dicendum mihi est Washingtonii, in ea scilicet urbe, cuius vel ipsum nomen gratae erga *patriae patrem* tot illustrissimae civitates, amicissimo inter se foedere coniunctae, peculiari quadam observantia prosequuntur; in sede reipublicae illius, quam sapientissimis legibus temperatam, mira civium in amplissima libertate industria, in maxima aemulatione concordia florentissimam, non modo ceterae Americae nationes, sed Europa etiam, totus denique orbis non sine quadam invidia admirabundi suspiciunt! Nonne tandem veterum illud: Ne Iliada post Homerum! Ne Olynthiam post Demosthenem! verissime quis mihi dictum putaverit, quippe qui verba ad vos facere ausim post oratores omnibus nominibus praestantissimos omnique exceptione maiores, quorum vox auctoritatis atque eloquentiae plena hisce ipsis diebus, quid dico? immo hoc ipso die, hac ipsa hora vestrum tantopere haud immerito plausum admirationemque excitavit? Quare non audaciae tantum, sed temeritatis

forem arguendus, si coram vobis, Eminentissimi, Reverendissimi, Ornatissimi auditores! dicendi munus ullo
modo appetivissem et si plura pluribus persequi in animo
esset. Cum vero in hunc locum non conscenderim nisi
iis impulsus precibus, quibus reniti nefas, iam ipsa haec
obsequentis atque obedientis erga insignem Rectorem
nostrum voluntatis significatio facile efficiet, ut pauca
dicturus nulla apud vos ·excusatione indigeam, et contra
eximia vestra benignitas atque humanitas meam non
mediocriter sublevet ac sustentet infirmitatem.

Quid prius dicam solitis Parentis
Laudibus?

Nam profecto, si ullo unquam post ereptos Americae
populos e paganitatis tenebris tempore cognitum atque
comprobatum fuit, quam paterna Deus O. M. nascentem
in his regionibus Ecclesiam suam providentia sit am·
plexus et adhuc amplectatur; quanta sit sanctissimae
religioni nostrae ad maxima quaeque suscipienda suscep-
taque perficienda, indita divinitus vis atque virtus: in iis
certe, quos per centum abhinc annos reportatos celebravi-
mus, triumphis; in novo hoc inusitatoque, quem hodie
agimus, ita haec omnia patefacta sunt, ut nunquam
maioribus et illustrioribus argumentis aut illustrata esse
aut in posterum illustrari posse videantur. Quapropter
ante omnia gratias iterum atque iterum persolvemus
praesenti praepotentique Numini, quo non aedificante
domum, in vanum laborant hominum vel ingeniosissima
consilia, "*a quo omne datum bonum et omne donum per-*

67

fectum mandatum est nobis in plenitudinem catholicae eius et apostolicae Ecclesiae."[1] Nos vero, quotquot, licet immeriti, ad optimos quosque adolescentes altioribus disciplinis informandos huc acciti sumus, fide sollemniter coram vobis, Patres amplissimi, data, nostrum illud perpetuo verbum [2] facimus : *"Deus lux mea!"* altissimisque radicibus in mentibus nostris defixa facem nobis in inquirendo atque docendo nunquam non praeferet magni Leonis XIII sententia; *"conatus nostros irritos futuros, nisi communia coepta Ille secundet, qui 'Deus scientiarum' in divinis eloquiis appellatur!"* [3]

IAM vero divini illius ac prorsus ineffabilis amoris, quo coelestis Paterfamilias omnes omnium caritates amplectitur unus, *"mensuram bonam et confertam et coagitatam et supereffluentem"* [4] dedit in sinum ILLIUS, quem ad gubernandam universam familiam suam [5] IN PETRI SEDE constituit quemque *Patrem* per orbem terrarum sancta colit atque veneratur Ecclesia.

Nemo tam Pater! hocce verissimo eodemque suavissimo elogio inde a primis rerum christianarum exordiis ad nostra usque tempora grati prosecuti sunt populi Romanos Pontifices, qui per Urbem et Orbem, per oppida et vicos, per tempora et saecula ad instar divini Magistri *"pertransierunt benefaciendo!"* [6]

Nemo tam Pater! sic in mirabili mundi totius concentu, tot tantorumque memor beneficiorum, Petri successores devota compellat America!

[1] *Cf.* Patres Concil. Lateran. sub Martino I.
[2] Encycl. Aeterni Patria.
[5] *Cf.* S. Ignat. M. ad Ephes.
[3] In aedificio insculptum.
[4] Luc. 6, 38.
[6] Act. 10, 38.

Nemo tam Pater! Sic te, Leo maxime, sollemni hoc faustissimoque die nostra haec laetabunda salutat academia!

Tu enim, teste dilectissimo Cardinali nostro, splendidissimo illo ecclesiae Americanae lumine, tu singulari tua sollicitudine atque prudentia "rigasti, quae Pius P. VI plantavit!"[1]

Tu tuae erga nos voluntatis illum nobis misisti interpretem, quo meliorem, doctiorem atque eloquentiorem non dico invenire, sed ne exoptare quidem potuissemus![2]

Liceat mihi, Illustrissime ac Reverendissime Summi Pastoris legate, carissimorum collegarum meisque verbis hanc abs te expetere gratiam, ut amantissimo Patri nostros filialis amoris atque obedientiae sensus aperias, quibus imbuti, nullo neglecto artium et scientiarum vero progressu, ex divinis humanisque thesauris "nova proferentes et vetera," Magni Aquinatis doctrinam "*illustrare, tueri et ad grassantium errorum refutationem adhibere*"[3] pro viribus conabimur. Totius vero nostrae credendi, agendi docendique rationis veluti tesseram quandam Divi Hieronymi luculentissima illa verba Supremo Iudici exhibeas: "*Nos nullum primum nisi Christum sequentes, Beatudini Tuae, i. e. Cathedrae Petri consociamur! Super illam aedificatam ecclesiam scimus! Non novimus falsitatis magistros, pravas opiniones respuimus, ignoramus novatores! Qui tecum non colligit, spargit. Si quis cathedrae Petri iungitur, noster est!*"[4]

---

[1] Emus Card. Gibbons in litteris pastoralibus.   [2] Sc. Rmum archiep. Satolli.
[3] Encycl. "Aeterni Patris." *Cf.* Constitutiones Catholicae Universitatis Americae, p. 42, 45.   [4] *Cf.* ep. 15. et 16. ad Damas.

SICUTI vero, ut S. Cypriani verbis utar, "*episcopatus unus est, cuius a singulis in solidum pars tenetur,*"[1] ita etiam laus tot fidei victoriis ac triumphis nostris in regionibus adepta, in EPISCOPOS redundat, quos in partem sollicitudinis a Romano Pontifice vocatos in nobis "*Spiritus Sanctus posuit regere ecclesiam Dei.*"[2] Quis vero in Americae historia tam est peregrinus atque hospes, qui quanta sint praesulum, quanta cleri populique Catholici universi in instituendo hoc Lycaeo merita, quot in perficiendo tanto opere difficultates fortiter superaverint, quot labores invicto animo exantlaverint, non legerit vel audiverit? Quis est tam remotus, tam inaccessus toto orbe locus, quo munificentissimae illius vereque regiae, quam pastores egregii verbo et exemplo in civibus non semel excitaverunt, liberalitatis fama non pervaserit?

In vos, Reverendissimi Praesules, Sancti Augustini, apostolicos priscae aetatis viros laudibus exornantis verba lubentissime transferam: "*Isti episcopi sunt, docti, graves, sancti, veritatis acerrimi defensores, in quorum ratione, eruditione, libertate, non potes invenire quod spernas. Talibus post Apostolos sancta Ecclesia plantatoribus, rigatoribus, aedificatoribus, pastoribus, nutritoribus crevit, qui divinae familiae dominica cibaria fideliter ministrantes ingenti in Domino gloria claruerunt.*"[3]

Salvete igitur, pastores eximii! Salvete americani gregis decora atque ornamenta! Salvete huius academiae firmamenta et praesidia! Vestram festis hisce diebus intuiti frequentissimam nobilissimamque coronam, ves-

---

[1] De unitate ecclesiae.   [2] Cf. Act. 20, 28.
[3] Cf. Aug. cont. Iul. II, n. 37.

tram admirati "*communicationem pacis et appellationem fraternitatis et contesserationem hospitalitatis,*"[1] non potuimus nostros cohibere summae laetitiae sensus; non potuimus non exclamare cum regio propheta: "*O quam bonum et quam iucundum habitare tales fratres in unum!*"

Vos igitur cum Petri Sede arctissimo vinculo coniunctos duces sequemur ac magistros; vestra nostra est laus, vester noster est honor. Patrum secuti exemplum "*intellectus secundum quem sentimus*"[2] tanquam arrabonem et pignus vobis esse volumus immotam illam "*fidei et sanitatis regulam:*"[3] "*Communicamus cum successoribus Apostolorum, communicamus cum episcopis nostris, quod nulli doctrina diversa: hoc est testimonium veritatis!*"[4]

QUID tandem quod non catholicos tantum, sed omnes harum civitatum cives, quod universam hanc potentissimam rempublicam uberrimos ex hisce Ecclesiae Catholicae triumphis fructus esse percepturos, meo mihi iure dicere posse videor? Immortale enim Dei miserentis opus, quod est Ecclesia, eaque ex materno ipsius sinu efflorescunt instituta, quamquam per se et natura sua salutem spectant animorum adipiscendamque in coelis felicitatem, tamen in ipso etiam rerum mortalium genere tot ac tantas ultro pariunt utilitates, ut plures maioresve non possent, si in primis et maxime essent ad tuendam huius vitae, quae in terris agitur, prosperitatem destinata.[5] Quid vero hac in re verbis opus est,

---

[1] Tertull. Praescript. c. 20, 21.   [2] S. Athanas. or. I cont. Arian. n. 34.
[3] S. August. in Ioann. tract. 18 n. 1.   [4] *Cf.* Tertull. Praescript. l. c.
[5] *Cf.* Leonis PP. XIII Encycl, de civitatum constitutione christiana.

cum facta quodammodo loqui videantur? Nonne hanc ipsam ob causam summi illi viri, qui ad reipublicae nostrae sedent gubernacula, hodiernum nostrum concessum exoptatissima sua praesentia cohonestarunt atque exornarunt? Nonne id ipsum persuasum est innumeris illis civibus nostris, qui, licet aliter de rebus divinis sentiant, insignis tamen suae erga nos benevolentiae et existimationis haud ambigua signa tum antea praestiterunt tum hoc quoque die praestare non dubitant?

Augeatur igitur et crescat in hisce plagis, coelestibus benedictionibus quoquoversus repletis, sanctae religionis amor et reverentia!

Vivat et floreat, Dei O. M. auxilio innixa, Deiparae Immaculatae, S. Joseph, Divi Pauli, S. Thomae Coelitumque omnium patrocinio fulta, academia haec nostra, tam felicibus hodie auspiciis coepta!

Adolescant in ea et ad gravissimas quasque disciplinas exerceantur iuvenes ingenui, ut ad sacra praelia valentes quam qui maxime existant![1]

Clarius in dies clariusque generosissimis Americae populis orbique universo innotescat, quam vera sit, quam aperta, quam sincera sententia, aedium harum fronti marmoreis, cordibus vero nostris flammeis iisque nunquam interituris litteris inscripta: "DEO ET PATRIAE!"

Dixi.

---

[1] *Cf.* Leonis XIII. epist. ad episc. Bavariae.

72

Convenientque tuas avidi componere laudes
Undique, quique canunt vincto pede, quique soluto.
Tib.

Oh! mihi quae rerum spectacula laeta novarum
Nunc sese obiiciunt! quae nos delectat imago
Et mira attonitum replet dulcedine pectus!
Scilicet e vastis nostri confinibus orbis
Concilium, sanctique Patres, simul agmine facto,
Et clari coiere viri, quos inclita virtus
Divitiisque suis Sapientia diva magistros
Efficit, et partum sustollit ad aethera nomen.
Plaude, America, bonis summo quam spectat ab axe
Luminibus, laetisque Deus confirmat et auget
Auspiciis; mecumque, Viri, vos plaudite iunctis
Laetitiis, meliusque sacris confidite rebus.

Lux iam centenis convertitur orbibus anni,
Elapsoque dies fortunatissima saeclo
Iam redit, in nostris viguit quo condita terris
Religio et pietas, Pastoribus undique sacris
Legitimo proprias habitantibus ordine sedes,
Atque potestatis, Petri quae manat ab Urbe,
Per certos demum sancito iure ministros.

Quis fando memoret manibus quot munera plenis,
Quot benefacta Deus, tot iam volventibus annis,
Contulerit nobis? quam laetos usque triumphos,
Quot palmas, coelo victoria lapsa sereno,
Foedere perpetuo nostris effuderit oris?
Quam multis lux affulsit divinitus hausta!
Quam late Christi nomen cultusque per urbes
Montesque et silvas, ac per deserta ferarum
Emicuit, pressasque diu caligine gentes
Eripuit tenebris Christique adiunxit ovili!

Pax et amica quies nostris dominatur in agris.
Aurea libertas, quam lex tamen aequa coercet
Et regit imperio : foecundo copia cornu
Divitias sine fine parat ; prudentia rerum
Eximia hos populos cunctis regionibus aequat.
Impietas petulans magis usque magisque fatiscit ;
Errorum fera turba fugit ; fugere phalanges
Tartareae, et Stygii franguntur sceptra tyranni,
Dum quassat ventis insignia sacra secundis
Relligio, subigitque animos victricibus armis.

At nunc ecce novum, revoluto sidere, saeclum
Incipit, augurio natum meliore, novoque
Ordine, qui rebus ferat incrementa futuris
Et libertatis sanctae faustissima dona
Provehat in melius ; Christi sacri iura propaget,
Clarius et veri collustret lumine mentes.
Omine propitio superisque iuvantibus, ALMA
Consurgit SEDES, studiisque volentibus ardet
Tutari sacras coniunctis viribus artes,
Iustitiam legesque pias, exemplaque vitae
Quae gentes reddant terraque poloque beatas,
Et quidquid ratio, quidquid pia dogmata tradunt
Christicolum sanas docuisse fideliter aures.

Sic Deus aspiret coeptis, et Virgo secundet
Consilium, ut mulcet spes iucundissima pectus :
Affore mox tempus, plenam sapientia lucem
Cum terris America tuis pelagoque refundet,
Et Christi imperium cunctis dominabitur oris.
Hoc omnes cupimus : vult hoc Leo maximus, afflat
Qui primus tantos generosa in pectora sensus ;
Et quamquam pressus bello vinctusque catenis,

Proh ! scelus et probrum ! tamen omnia circumspectat
Impiger, et populos toto procul orbe remotos
Sublevat auxilio, cunctasque informat ad artes.

. Salve, Magne Pater ! duce te, teque auspice surgat
Hoc opus, et fructus in longum proferat aevum !
Et quae consilio, virtute, et fortibus ausis
Iamdudum floret, doctrinae floreat haustu
Religione potens pietate AMERICA refulgens,
Et servet magni nomen per saecla LEONIS.

When the applause which followed Mgr. Schroeder's
eloquent address had subsided, a full choir chanted the
OREMUS PRO PONTIFICE NOSTRO LEONE; Cardinal Gibbons gave his benediction, and the exercises of the
Inauguration Day of the Catholic University of America
were at an end.

Ere the vast multitude of guests and visitors had
begun to disperse, the storm-clouds, apt symbols of the
difficulties inseparable from the beginnings of such an
enterprise, had rolled away, and the evening stars shone
down clear and tranquil from a cloudless sky, fit type
of the placid routine of University life that was now to
begin within the walls which this day had consecrated
to Religion and Science.

THE ACTUAL OPENING OF UNIVERSITY WORK.

That very evening, at half past eight o'clock, the first corps of students assembled in the University Chapel, to begin their spiritual retreat. During the four following days, the exercises of this holy time of recollection and prayer, conducted by the Rt. Rev. Rector and the Rev. Father Hogan, S. S., were carried on as calmly and regularly as if the institution had been years in existence, and not just emerged from the bustle and ceremony of its inauguration.

On Monday morning, November 18th, the Rt. Rev. Rector celebrated the Mass of the Holy Ghost, in the presence of the entire Faculty and the students. At its close, the Professors of Divinity, kneeling before the altar, recited aloud the Profession of Catholic Faith, and kissed the Holy Gospels as a pledge of their faithful adhesion to the same in all their teaching. Professors and students together then chanted the *Te Deum* with splendid effect.

A few minutes later, all were assembled in one of the lecture halls, to hear the opening discourse, delivered by the Rt. Rev. Rector.

He began by showing the relation between the course of study which they had made in the various Seminaries, and that which they were now to begin in the University; which, he explained, was to be deeper, broader, and more practically applied to all the questions agitating the mind of the world to-day. He introduced to the students successively the Professors of Dogmatic Theology, of Moral Theology, of Apologetics or Fundamental Theology, of Holy Scripture, and of English Literature, and sketched the course of instruction which each was to give during the year, as had been determined in previous meetings of the Faculty and of the University Senate. He indicated the order in which there were soon to be added courses of Sacred Eloquence and of Elocution, of the Scriptural and modern languages, and of other branches accessory to sacred studies. He dwelt upon the spirit of manly earnestness and dutifulness which success in such work would demand from them, and expressed his conviction that, in all the qualities which make model students, this first corps, the pioneers of the great work, would be a pattern and a mould for all the generations of students that were to follow them.

The enthusiasm of their response proved that the appeal and the confidence should not be in vain. The remainder of the day was spent in recreation, and in immediate preparation for the scholastic duties at hand.

The following day, Tuesday, November 19th, each of the Professors held class, and work was begun in earnest.

V.

PERSONNEL OF THE UNIVERSITY AND COURSES OF INSTRUCTION GIVEN.

THE BOARD OF DIRECTORS.

The Board of Directors, who are also the legal trustees of the University Corporation, are the following:

His Eminence, James Cardinal Gibbons, *Archbishop of Baltimore, Chancellor of the University.*

The Most Rev. J. J. Williams, D. D., *Archbishop of Boston.*

  "   "   "   M. A. Corrigan, D. D.,   "   *New York.*

  "   "   "   P. J. Ryan, D. D.,   "   *Philadelphia.*

  "   "   "   John Ireland, D. D.,   "   *St. Paul.*

  " Right "   Camillus P. Maes, D. D., *Bishop of Covington.*

  "   "   "   John Foley, D. D.,   "   *Detroit.*

  "   "   "   Kilian C. Flasch, D. D.,   "   *La Crosse.*

  "   "   "   J. L. Spalding, D. D.,   "   *Peoria.*

  "   "   "   M. Marty, D. D., O. S. B.,   "   *Sioux Falls.*

  "   "   "   John J. Keane, D. D., *Rector.*

  " Very "   Mgr. J. M. Farley, *New York.*

  " Rev. P. L. Chapelle, D. D., *Washington, D. C.*

  " " Thomas Lee, *Baltimore.*

78

Mr. Eugene Kelly, *Treasurer, New York.*
" Michael Jenkins, *Baltimore.*
" Thos. E. Waggaman, *Washington.*

OFFICIALS AND PROFESSORS.

Rt. Rev. John J. Keane, D. D., *Bishop of Ajasso, Rector:* directs
the administration of the University; lectures on Sacred Eloquence.

Rev. Philip J. Garrigan, D. D., *Vice-Rector:* has charge of the
business management of the institution.

Very Rev. John B. Hogan, S. S., D. D.: directs the ecclesiastical
discipline of the Divinity College; lectures three times a week
on Ascetical Theology.

Rev. A. Orban, S. S., *Librarian:* assistant director of ecclesiastical
discipline; conducts private classes of Geology.

Very Rev. Monsignor Joseph Schroeder, D. D., *Professor of
Dogmatic Theology, Dean of the Faculty:* lectures four times a
week,—during the first few weeks, *Introductio in Theologiam, seu
Commentarius in I. p., q. I., Summae S. Thomae;* after Christ-
mas, *De objectivis Fidei principiis, nominatim de Traditione et
Scriptura. Commentarius in Constit. I. Concilii Vaticani.*

Rev. Thomas Bouquillon, D. D., *Professor of Fundamental Moral
Theology:* lectures four times a week,—during the first term,
Introductio Generalis in Theologiam Moralem; second term,
De Actibus Humanis.

Rev. Joseph Pohle, D. D., *Professor of Christian Apologetics or
the Philosophical Foundations of Religion:* lectures four times
a week,—during the first term, *De existentia et attributis
Dei;* during the second term, *De spiritualitate et immortalitate
animae.*

REV. HENRY HYVERNAT, D. D., *Professor of Scriptural Archæology and Oriental Languages:* lectures twice a week on Scriptural Archæology ; and twice a week, during the first term, on Hebrew, during the second term, on Syriac.

REV. JOSEPH GRAF, *Choir-Master*, gives classes and private lessons in Liturgical Chant.

MR. CHARLES WARREN STODDARD, *Lecturer on English Literature:* conducts weekly courses of literary criticism.

MONS. BAZERQUE, holds frequent classes in the French language and literature.

PROFESSOR WEBSTER EDGERLY, gives weekly classes in Elocution.

LECTURERS.

A notable feature in the contemplated plan are the popular discourses known as the CATHOLIC UNIVERSITY LECTURES. It is intended that in these lectures questions of scientific interest or practical importance shall be treated by able men, whether of the Faculty or not, learnedly indeed, yet so as to be within the grasp of ordinarily intelligent minds. They are to be given on two afternoons in every week, usually in English, but occasionally in French, German, or other languages. While meant primarily for the improvement of the students, they are to be free to the public, and thus will give to reflective persons of all creeds an opportunity of hearing living and important questions ably treated from a Catholic stand-point.

These were inaugurated, on November 20th, with a series of nine lectures by the VERY REV. AUGUSTINE F. HEWIT, D. D., on *the Catholic Idea of the Church, in Scripture and in Antiquity.*

Rev. P. L. Chapelle, D. D., will lecture on *the Typical Personages of Patristic History,* in a series of six or eight discourses.

Rev. George M. Searle, C. S. P., will lecture throughout the year on *Astronomy and Mathematics.*

The Professors will take part in the course, lecturing on subjects kindred to their specialties, and other speakers distinguished in literature and science will carry it on throughout the year. Special announcement is to be made at the beginning of each month of the lectures to be given during it. The following announcements for January, 1890, may serve to illustrate the nature of this part of the work:

Wednesday, Jan. 8th, Professor Schroeder: *Der Pessimismus, oder die philosophischen Schwarzseher.*

" " 15th, Professor Bouquillon: *L'origine des droits de l'homme.*

" " 22d, Professor Pohle: *John Stuart Mill on Theism.*

" " 29th, Bishop Keane: *Herbert Spencer's "First Principles."*

On the Fridays in January, a series of Lectures on *Astronomy,* by Rev. George M. Searle, as follows:

Friday, Jan. 10th, *Introductory. Apparent motions of the celestial sphere and of the principal heavenly bodies.*

" " 17th, *Shape, size, and rotation of the earth.*

" " 24th, *Distance, dimensions, and physical constitution of the sun.*

" " 31st, *Light and heat of the sun.*

PROFESSORS ABROAD.

Provision is made for enlarging the Faculty of Divinity, and for laying the foundations of other Faculties, by securing the services of men distinguished for their intellectual acquirements, and, if possible, already noted for success in teaching, and allowing them the advantages offered by the European Universities before they begin their work at home. Four of our future Professors are thus engaged at present:

REV. THOMAS J. SHAHAN, D. D., of Hartford, Conn., is pursuing historical studies in Berlin.

REV. EDWARD A. PACE, D. D., of St. Augustine, Fla., is finishing a course of anthropology at Leipzig.

REV. SEBASTIAN MESSMER, D. D., is perfecting the study of Canon Law in Rome.

REV. CHARLES GRANNAN, D. D., of New York, is in Paris, engaged in Scriptural studies.

THE STUDENTS.

The studies of the Divinity Faculty being those of a strictly University course, presupposing the full College and Seminary course of Classics, Philosophy, and Theology, the students are nearly all Priests, some having been ordained when leaving their Seminaries for the University, others having spent from one to ten years

in the exercise of the holy ministry. The following is
the list of the first corps of students:

REV. GEORGE GLAAB............*Of the Archdiocese of Baltimore.*
" WM. A. FLETCHER........ " " "
" T. E. GALLAGHER........ " " "
MR. J. C. FITZGERALD.......... " " "
REV. FRANCIS J. BUTLER....... " " *Boston.*
" J. C. McGOLDRICK........ " " "
" J. B. LABOSSIERE......... " " "
" T. J. WHALEN............. " " *Chicago.*
" D. McCAFFREY .... " " "
" M. MULVEHILL............. " " *Cincinnati.*
" D. J. O'HEARN............. " " *Milwaukee.*
" WM. C. KELLY............ " " *New York.*
" JAMES FITZSIMMONS....... " " "
" J. T. HIGGINS .... " " *Philadelphia.*
" JAMES CARROLL........... " " "
" M. J. CRANE.............. " " "
" J. F. TUOHY .... " " *St. Louis.*
" P. J. DANEHY............. " " *St. Paul.*
" J. F. BUSCH................ " " "
" PETER YORKE.............. " " *San Francisco.*
" J. J. DRISCOLL................*Of the Diocese of Albany.*
" JOS. P. McGINLEY............. " " *Brooklyn.*
MR. R. C. O'CONNELL................. " " *Buffalo.*
" J. F. MOONEY..................... " " "
REV. W. S. KRESS..................... " " *Cleveland.*
" FREDERICK RUPERT........... " " "
" J. J. LOFTUS..................... " " *Hartford.*
MR. D. BROWN .... " " "
" H. R. McCABE..................... " " *Marquette.*
REV. J. F. SULLIVAN.................. " " *Providence.*

MR. A. L. McNULTY	*Of the Diocese of Sioux Falls.*		
REV. J. C. IVERS	"	"	*Springfield.*
" J. P. McCAUGHAN	"	"	"
" W. J. FITZGERALD	"	"	*Trenton.*
" S. M. WIEST, S. P. M	"	"	"
" JOHN STANTON	"	"	*Vincennes.*
" L. BESNARD	*Of the Society of St. Sulpice.*		

Nine students of the Congregation of St. Paul the Apostle reside in St. Thomas's College, adjoining the University, and attend several of the courses.

Places have been secured for two students of the Diocese of Detroit, not yet entered.

Some of the neighboring Clergy have declared their intention to attend various classes.

VI

THE FOUNDERS OF PROFESSORIAL CHAIRS.

In this official account of the opening of the University, it is deemed proper to make mention of those to whose generosity the success thus far accomplished is mainly due.

First among these is Miss Mary Gwendolen Byrd Caldwell, whose munificent gift of three hundred thousand dollars laid the foundation of the whole work. In this splendid act, her oft-declared desire was to erect a monument of thanksgiving to Almighty God for the grace of the Catholic Faith granted to her father and mother. Accordingly, she set apart one hundred thousand dollars of the amount for the perpetual endowment of two Professorial Chairs, to be forever designated by their names.

Her father's name is given to THE SHAKESPEARE CALDWELL CHAIR OF DOGMATIC THEOLOGY. It is a lasting and worthy monument to the noble character and stainless life of a true Christian gentleman. Through his mother, Shakespeare Caldwell was related to the Carters and Byrds of Virginia, thus belonging to the most highly respected families of the Old Dominion. In face and

84

person he was considered a model of manly beauty, in character a pattern of chivalrous honor, while his piety and charity as a Christian showed how highly he appreciated the grace of the Catholic Faith. This may be considered a family trait, the generous charity of his sister Sophia being shown by the fact that her name is borne by the Home of the Little Sisters of the Poor in Richmond.

Miss Caldwell's mother has for her special monument THE ELIZABETH BRECKENRIDGE CALDWELL CHAIR OF PHILOSOPHY. This distinguished lady, daughter of James Breckenridge of Louisville, Ky., sprang from a family noted among the oldest and best in Kentucky for intellectual ability and strength of character. Both of these qualities she inherited in a remarkable degree. But far beyond all considerations of pedigree she valued the priceless gift of the Apostolic Faith, which she believed to have been bestowed upon her almost miraculously. In no way could her worth be more fittingly commemorated than by thus inseparably associating her name with an institution in which Divine Faith is forever to be intimately linked with human learning.

From both their parents the Misses Caldwell have received the double inheritance of an honorably acquired fortune and a lovingly cherished faith. They have proved themselves worthy of both by the noble part which they have taken in the establishment of the University, the younger sister, Miss Elizabeth Breckenridge Caldwell, having donated the fifty thousand dollars which have erected and adorned the beautiful Divinity Chapel.

The first to emulate this example of generosity and filial devotedness were the Misses Andrews of Baltimore, who, in memory of their venerated father, endowed THE ANDREWS CHAIR OF SCRIPTURAL ARCHÆOLOGY. We are indebted to the pen of one who knew him well for the following account of this remarkable man:

SKETCH OF THE LIFE OF DR. THOMAS F. ANDREWS.

The late Dr. Thomas Francis Andrews was for many years an eminent citizen of Virginia. Indeed the city of Norfolk never produced a more gifted and cultivated man, although it was the birthplace of distinguished lawyers and scholars of that day, as well as the centre of a brilliant and charming society.

The father of Dr. Andrews was English by birth; his mother was a Miss Lynch, from the south of Ireland, a near relative of the well-known Lynches of Virginia and Maryland, aunt of Lieutenant Lynch, the Dead Sea explorer, who was afterwards Commodore in the Confederate Navy. They settled in Norfolk, where the subject of our sketch was born on the 19th day of March, 1797.

At an early age he had the misfortune to lose his mother, and was himself during childhood frequently under the care of physicians. When of an age to choose a profession, he selected medicine, which he studied under Dr. Fernandez, then practicing in Norfolk. This gentleman was known in his own country by the name of Oliveira; he had been physician to the King of Portugal, was exiled for some years through a court intrigue, but

was afterwards recalled to high honors in his native land.
The father of young Andrews sent him to Europe to
pursue his studies in Paris, Berlin, and lastly at the
University of Edinburgh, where he graduated with distinction.   He then resided for a time in London, pursuing
his profession there, but returned home to inherit the
practice of Dr. Fernandez, upon the recall of the latter to
the Court of Portugal.   From this time onward, for thirty
years and more, Dr. Andrews lived in Norfolk, honored,
admired, trusted and beloved by the entire community.

Failing health, in the full tide of his professional
supremacy, compelled him to remove from his home; it
was found impossible to retire from practice, while dwell-
ing in the midst of a people who would not consent to
relinquish his services.   He had acquired a sufficient
fortune; and for a series of years he travelled in Europe,
Egypt, and the Holy Land.   Although he never resumed
practice, he occasionally joined in consultations when
invited by other physicians both in Europe and this
country.   Upon his return to the United States, he spent
some time in Washington and Georgetown, afterwards in
Baltimore, where he died on the 21st of January, 1886.
He was interred in the family vault in the Catholic Ceme-
tery of Norfolk; the faithful companion of his life, one
son and two daughters surviving him.

It is in Norfolk, the place of his nativity and marriage,
and the resting-place of his earthly remains, that the
fame of Dr. Andrews is proudly and affectionately cherished as an heirloom.   Here was the scene of his triumphs,
and not merely in the field of science.   During the

administration of General Jackson, who was united to him by the ties that such men love to appreciate, Dr. Andrews was in the front rank of the Democratic party in his District. His profound mastery of political economy, and his skill as a financier, qualified him in the universal estimation, for high distinction in the public service. But he was content to be loved by his own people. To them he was always the matchless physician, the wise counsellor, the true friend, the delightful companion and the flashing wit; for this distinguished and eminently useful man was unquestionably the most brilliant conversationalist of all his cotemporaries. One of his life-long friends, the late William Willoughby Sharp, of the Norfolk Bar, who was also intimately associated with the renowned debater, Governor Tazewell, has left this testimony: "Andrews was the only man I ever met who, in a colloquial encounter with Governor Tazewell, could withstand his ingenuity and power." And that was but one aspect of his genius.

Above all he was an upright gentleman, unselfish, kind-hearted, sympathetic, liberal in his charities, whether in the temporary gift or in the long sustained aid of years, faithful in every relation to his family, to the extended circle of his friends, and to the State which, throughout his life, he honored and revered with a patriot's love.

The Misses Drexel, renowned throughout the country and the world for their generous coöperation in the Church's works of charity and of zeal, were not slow to take part in what the highest ecclesiastical authorities have declared to be the most important work that the Church has yet undertaken in America. As an evidence of their appreciation and sympathy, they have endowed a Professorial Chair, which, as a perpetual monument to their beloved and honored father, shall be known as THE FRANCIS A. DREXEL CHAIR OF MORAL THEOLOGY. We are happy to give the following biographical notice of this model Christian gentleman, written by a friend of many years.

A SKETCH OF THE LIFE OF FRANCIS ANTHONY DREXEL as it is known to the world, can be placed in a very narrow frame-work of dates and facts. Born in Philadelphia in the year 1824, he was the eldest son of Francis M. Drexel, who had emigrated from the Tyrol in one of the early decades of this century; and I may here mention, that the only occasion on which the writer of this record witnessed a marked deviation from the ordinary quiet, reflective manner of the son was when, at a dinner-table, casual mention was made of the Tyrolese patriot, Andrew Hofer, the hero of his father's native land. I have heard that the motive for the original departure of the Drexel family from the Tyrol—a country that thrusts few of her children from her bosom—was supplied by their implication in the struggle against Napoleon for national independence, and the maintenance of fidelity to Austria. This, however, I have no present means of verifying.

Francis A. Drexel was associated with his father in the early days when the broad foundations of what are now known as the Drexel Banks were laid; and it is in no small measure to his quick insight, prompt judgment and profound sagacity, acquired and developed in the counting-house at that time, that they are indebted for their present high and secure position in the financial world. Yet, though he spent his youth in the discharge of duties generally held to conflict with the acquirement of scholarly tastes, Mr. Drexel had, in riper years at least, accumulated large stores of scientific knowledge gained by close observation, and systematized by undesultory reading.

Refined in tastes, pure in morals, simple in manners, warm in his friendships, happy in the retired life into which so much domestic affection was garnered, there is little to be related of his career that would either dazzle or fascinate. But were a faithful and minute record of the *inner* life of Francis A. Drexel given, few biographies would be more conducive to edification. As was said by one of his contemporaries, "To consider him truly was *not* to consider him as a man of business, but as a man of charity;" and I will add of Christian charity, the outcome, not of restlessness, unutilized energies, or ambition, but of deep religious convictions.

Mr. Drexel's faith was laid in strong, well-defined lines, and its practical influence was made manifest in habitual esteem for all things sacred, and in his frequent and reverent approach to the Holy Table. It may not be amiss to say here, that this man, immersed in enterprises of world-wide extent, found time for daily spiritual reading, and for a monthly reception of the Sacraments, which was always accompanied by a three days' preparation and a three days' thanksgiving.

This is as much of his history as we are concerned
with. Many of his benefactions are written in the chron-
icles of the Religious Communities and Charitable Institutions of his country; but the hundreds who have been
the beneficiaries of his private, unrecorded charities will
never be known on earth.

Not on earth, either, will be known the influence
towards what was best, exercised by the great-souled
woman, the wife who coöperated with him in all his work
for the benefit of others, and who was, indeed, until her
death, two years before his own, largely the administra-
trix of *his* bounties. What is not possible to the rich man
whose wife's motto is, " We are God's Almoners"?

On the 29th of January, 1883, this wife passed to her
reward. On February 15th, 1885, Francis A. Drexel
entered into that Kingdom where he had laid up his
treasures.

The venerable Treasurer of the University, Mr. Eugene
Kelly of New York, to whose wise practical counsels the
Board of Directors have been, from the very beginning,
largely indebted for the success of their administration,
has moreover associated his name forever with the work
of the University by the endowment of a Chair, to be
known as THE EUGENE KELLY CHAIR OF ECCLESIASTI-
CAL HISTORY.

His excellent wife, universally honored for all the
qualities which constitute the true Christian lady, whose
name tells of her relationship to the great Archbishop of
New York, has imitated the noble act of her husband,

and has endowed THE MARGARET HUGHES KELLY CHAIR OF SCRIPTURAL EXEGESIS.

Among the men who have most contributed to the solid progress of the Pacific Coast, none stands more highly respected for public-spirited activity, for irreproachable honor, for Christian character, than the Hon. Myles P. O'Connor, of San Jose, California. He has shown his appreciation of this crowning work of Christian Education by endowing THE O'CONNOR CHAIR OF CANON LAW.

The CATHOLIC TOTAL ABSTINENCE UNION OF AMERICA has held an honorable position, for nearly twenty years, among the organizations which have successfully labored for the moral and social elevation of the Catholics of the United States. The Centenary of their illustrious Patron and Model, the great and good Father Theobald Matthew, comes in 1890. As the most worthy monument that they could erect to this saintly priest and eminent benefactor of mankind, the Union has resolved to endow a Chair in the University, to be forever distinguished by the name of THE FATHER MATTHEW CHAIR.

The Catholics of the United States have long felt the propriety and duty of erecting a suitable monument to commemorate the wonderful learning and noble character of DR. ORESTES BROWNSON, who, during his long and spotless career, did more than all the other Catholic writers of America to make the Church known and honored by the people of our country. To reflective minds it was obvious that the memorial to such a man should in some way be connected with our central seat of Catholic learning. Accordingly, the project has been widely discussed of either erecting a monument to the great philosopher within the University grounds, or endowing a BROWNSON CHAIR as a still more suitable tribute to his genius. Upon either of these projects the authorities of the University would look with special favor, and it is hoped that in some shape this evident duty to a peerless name may soon be fulfilled.

Besides the founders of Professorial Chairs, it is deemed a duty of justice, as it is a great pleasure, to make special mention of four among the contributors to the establishment of the University, whose generosity has been the most notable. These are MR. PATRICK QUINN of Philadelphia, who gave $20,000; Mrs. William Reynolds, of the same city, who contributed $10,000; the family of Mr. Leopold Huffer, of Paris, France, who gave $8,000; and Mr. Sylvester Johnson, of Louisville, Ky., lately deceased, who, having given $5,000 during his life, left $10,000 more to the work in his last will.

VII

NEEDS AND PLANS FOR THE IMMEDIATE FUTURE.

THE LIBRARY.

One of the first cares of every institution of learning is to build up its library. With us it is naturally an object of special attention and solicitude. A good beginning has already been made. A special committee, under the chairmanship of the Most Rev. Archbishop of New York, have carefully superintended the purchase of five thousand dollars' worth of standard works of Divinity. To these the Most Rev. Chairman has added, as his personal gift, a splendid collection of the Greek and Latin Patrology. The first donation to the Library was a most interesting and valuable compilation of all the documents appertaining to the Council of the Vatican, bound in twenty-three volumes, presented by the Rev. Theodore Metcalf of Boston, who was one of the amanuenses of the Council. The most notable gift is that of the Rt. Rev. M. J. O'Farrell, Bishop of Trenton, who has presented three thousand volumes, mostly pertaining to Scripture, Theology, and History. The Rev. Dr.

Messmer has donated the *Decisiones Rotae Romanae*, a splendid collection of one hundred and twenty-one folio volumes.

Large sums must be spent for several years to come, to make the Library at all equal to the requirements of such an institution. And very considerable sums will be needed in order to properly locate the Library. The present quarters, under the Chapel, are only temporary, and are entirely too limited and in many ways unsuitable. A separate fire-proof building must, of course, be eventually erected for the University Library. But even for the special Library of the Divinity Faculty more appropriate quarters must speedily be provided, and this will depend upon the improvement next to be mentioned.

THE SOUTH WING.

Every portion of the present Divinity Building is already in use. There are rooms for only three more students; whereas there ought to be accommodations for the larger numbers of students who are sure to come from all parts of the country, and for the lodging of Clergymen who may at any time come to spend even a few days or a few weeks in the atmosphere of such a home of sacred learning. To supply this need, provision has been made in the plan of the building for the construction of an extensive south wing. On the lower floor, besides the Divinity Library and Reading-Room,

necessity of which has been mentioned above, there
ld be the Museum of Scriptural Archæology, which
now very limited temporary quarters in a class-room.
space thus occupied at present might then be given
to the collections of geology and anthropology, of
ch a beginning has already been made by friends of
University, and especially by Mr. Joseph Willcox of
ladelphia and Dr. Ouchterlony of Louisville, Ky.
se will be gradually increased, while we await the
ctures to be called for in the future by the depart-
ts of science.

he stories above the Library and Museum would
nish all the additional accommodations for professors
students which the Faculty of Divinity would be apt
equire. Nay it has been suggested that they might
porarily be occupied by the first lay students of the
iversity, to provide for whom is the object which the
ectors now have the nearest at heart.

THE NEXT FACULTY.

HEN SHALL THE COURSES BE OPENED FOR LAY STUDENTS?
rom the preceding report it is manifest that the
holic University of America has started on its career
h the most important of all its Faculties solidly estab-
ed. Within two years, the Divinity course will be
roughly organized,—the essential foundation of any

complete system of university education which aims at being Christian.

It is a great work accomplished in a short time. But the work cannot halt there, even for a while. The erection of the superstructure must be pushed on steadily.

It is a matter of deep thankfulness to Divine Providence that the means of university training for the Clergy should at last have been provided, fulfilling the wishes and prayers of those who laid in our country the foundations of the Church's prosperity. But we should be untrue to them and to the great interests in our hands, did we not hasten to give the work the extension which the welfare of Church and country imperatively demands, by placing its advantages within the reach of the laity as well. To do this as speedily as possible is the ardent desire of the authorities of the University, and of the Bishops of the United States, whom they represent. The responsibility of its being accomplished must lie with those in whose hands Providence has placed the pecuniary means by which alone it can be done. To these agents, therefore, of Divine Providence,—to those to whom God and the Church must look for the carrying on of this all-important work,—these closing lines are addressed.

Catholic educators in all parts of the country clearly recognize the need of a central seat of higher or post-graduate instruction. The young man who, at the age of 19 or 20, has taken his degree of A. B., and who is not in a hurry to throw away his books and enter the race for pelf, needs to pass to other surroundings, to an

lectual atmosphere different from that of his youth-
ollege life, where, upon a higher level, he may feel
all things conspire to make of him a cultured man,
rious scholar. Some such youths our colleges are
dy producing; and the very presence of such an
lectual goal before them would increase the number
easurably. It is the services of just such men that
ch and country will sorely need in the very near
e, and to provide means for their right development
e most imperative duty now weighing upon us.

ie sort of training which such men require is mostly
n in what is known as the Faculty of Philosophy and
ers. This comprises the extensive field of deep but
exactly professional studies, logical, metaphysical,
ary, historical, social, and scientific, which alone can
e a man a true scholar, a safe thinker, a useful
r, no matter what his profession or avocation may be.
e desire to begin, at the earliest possible day, the
nization of such a Faculty of Philosophy and Letters.
ady we see much of the way before us. What is
ed is money. To make the University a success, we
establish this next Faculty, as we have established
preceding one, without debt on the buildings, and
the Professorial Chairs endowed. No one who
ts for a moment will need to be informed that even
gin this in proper shape will demand several hun-
thousand dollars.

ie friends of Christian Education are very many,
k God, and are constantly becoming more numerous.
moral and religious needs and dangers of our times

are beginning to appeal even to the most callous, and to force all right-minded people into our ranks. In the hands of those already awake to the importance of the cause, Divine Providence has placed abundant means to do all that need be done. The only question is, will their convictions rouse them to action? And will their action be characterized by generosity like to that of the many friends of learning throughout our country who have consecrated millions upon millions to University Education, even without Christianity in it? Surely our aim, that of infusing the fullest Christianity into the highest education, is a nobler one than they had before them, and ought to impel to nobler doing. It is to this that the voice of the Bishops and of the Vicar of Christ calls the friends of Christian Education. According to their response shall be our speed in meeting the great need before us. We desire and hope to be ready for lay students in two years. Will those who can if they will, step forward and say it shall be done?

FORM OF BEQUEST.

ive and bequeath unto 'The Catholic University
rica,' a corporation duly incorporated under the
the District of Columbia, the sum of _____."

www.ingramcontent.com/pod-product-compliance
Lightning Source LLC
Chambersburg PA
CBHW020804020726
47495CB00008B/2588